All the Pretty People

All the Pretty People

JACK S. SCOTT

A Joan Kahn BOOK

St. Martin's Press
New York

Design by Manuela Paul

Library of Congress Cataloging in Publication Data

Scott, Jack S.
    All the pretty people.

    "A Joan Kahn book."
    I. Title.
PR6069.C589A79   1984   823'.914   84-11754
ISBN 0-312-02006-6

First Edition
10 9 8 7 6 5 4 3 2 1

All *the* *Pretty* *People*

1

In June, the rains came. For three solid weeks out of the statutory four, every morning the whole country got up to it, every night it went to bed made glum and spiteful by it. Mist shrouded the hills around the town, and in the puddled and pitted streets people splashed about complaining bitterly that it was more like bloody October. And how right they were. On the night when Detective Inspector Alfred Stanley Rosher squatted on a roof in his black hat and battleship grey raincoat, with his boxy-toed shoes bracing him against a low parapet, no little green man from Mars would ever have believed he had arrived on the sunny side of Harvest Festival.

It was cold, too, up on that roof. Detective Inspector Rosher said to the naked young man crouched further along, on top of the parapet: "Now come on, son—nobody's going to hurt you."

"Hurt me?" the young man cried. There was nothing unhappy about him. On the contrary, he radiated. "Who can hurt me? I am the One, the only Son of God. Who shall hurt me? He holds me in the hollow of His hand!"

"That's what I said," Rosher told him. "Nobody's going to hurt you." He stole a cautious inch toward the boy.

"Don't come any nearer," the lad cried. "I cannot allow you to touch me. I shall cast myself off, and fly. Up to my Father. Which art in Heaven."

"Yes," said Rosher. "Mm. Well, of course, you could do

that." The fire brigade craned among the people below, with a body-catcher spread. But it is dodgy work, catching bodies that do not come from a definite point, jumping straight. The young man had run up and down the parapet several times before Rosher came up ten minutes ago. "On the other hand, we could all go down and talk it over. With a nice hot cup of tea."

A reasonable approach. For the full ten minutes, the inspector had been very reasonable.

The young man was shivering, his nakedness gleaming with droplets. But he cried: "Get thou behind me! Satan and son of Satan!" He dropped his voice, to speak confidentially. "You know what's happening, don't you? My Father has sent a flood. Yea, the waters shall cover the earth, they will drown in their sins like dogs in their vomit. It's not the first time, you know. Remember Noah?"

"Uh-huh," said Inspector Rosher. When he inclined his head, water ran in a small stream from the brim of his hat. "Long time ago, though, that was."

"Oh yes. Yes. You've had time, haven't you? You've had time to sink the world deeper into sin." The lad pointed a shivering finger. "Satan! But you are vanquished! I have overcome death!" All this in a pleasant, conversational manner. And an educated accent.

"Look," the inspector said, "you can't save the world all on your own up here. Let's go down. We'll hire a hall—you can talk to all the people—"

"Talk?" the young man cried. "The time for talk is past! I must leave this world, I must fly to my Father." He stood up, tall and beautiful, with the thin, shining beauty of youth.

Keep him here, Rosher's mind said urgently. If he's going, keep him here as long as you can, hope they have time to get the net right under. He stole a foot or more as the lad stretched out his arms, lifting his streaming, handsome face to the dirty-yellow sky as he cried exultantly: "It is finished! Father—I come, I come!" He bent his knees, arms coming back to the position a swimmer assumes just before he dives; his face still exulting upward.

Rosher sprang. No, no—there was no room for that, no purchase for it. To try it would have sent him and the young man both straight over the edge. Somehow he hurled himself sideways; somehow he flung out an arm as he tumbled safe behind the parapet, one of those long, powerful and hairy arms that helped so much, especially when he was on the move, to give him the look of a bandy gorilla. One clutching hand fastened to a bare leg just below the knee and jerked back hard, bringing the naked body down on top of him. The lad snarled, fighting to free himself, but the inspector's grip had shifted. He had both arms wrapped around the legs now and as the struggle brought the soft and vulnerable testicles against his hand, he enclosed them and squeezed. No conscious thought was needed to guide Rosher in the way he should go, once physical combat was joined. There was scrambling now on the roof tiles above, the man he left at the skylight coming down to help.

Now the young man lifted his head and howled in something different from exultation, because a sharply squeezed testicle will divert a veritable saint from his ecstacy. This is what Rosher wanted, this convulsive rising up that freed his right arm and the mighty Hammer which made of him, in his salad day, All England Police boxing champion, three years running. Heavyweight division.

He could not swing it properly, of course; but it landed somewhere on the lad's cheekbone with sufficient force to stun for a second; and this was long enough. The constable who came up with Rosher was here now pinning the body flat, back from the parapet; holding the lad while somebody else slid down from the skylight, with free hands for snapping the cuffs on wrists forced behind the fine back.

Freed from under that wet, naked weight, Rosher picked up his hat and resettled it on a remarkably simian brow. "All right," he said. "Get 'em on his ankles, too. Then let's have him downstairs." He looked over the parapet, to wave a signal to those waiting below. Jesus Christ, he thought—it's a bloody long way down.

3

* * *

In the hours and days that followed, Inspector Rosher got to know a good deal about this lad scooped from a rooming-house roof. Probing is the essence of the job. What he did not know was that he would meet him again in October, in weather people said was just like June, lying dead in a woodland clearing. Murder. Not the slightest doubt about it.

2

On the beautiful morning following the evening when the lad was found in the wooded area five miles from the town, Inspector Rosher stood with Detective Sergeant Henry Panton on the doorstep of a rather nice detached house in the nearby village of Hutton Fellows. He had been up for most of the night, as had the many other officers called out immediately when the body was discovered by a lady jogger, but as yet he felt no strain. C.I.D. men are used to missing sleep. Weariness comes late, in the form of depressed reaction when the job is cleared or snarls up and must be put aside as unsolvable for the nonce. No murder file is ever closed officially; but Jack the Ripper has been hanging about for years.

It really was a beautiful morning. Even Rosher appreciated the crisp blueness of it as he rang the bell and gazed around at the well-tended garden where a few late roses still bloomed, asters and Michaelmas daisies and the optimistic chrysanthemums that bud and bloom and are savagely murdered year after year, blackened into stark ugliness by the first vicious frosts. Chrysanthemums never learn. "Keeps a nice garden," he remarked to Sergeant Panton as they waited under the neat porch.

"It's a nice house," the sergeant said. And it was. Modern, but not outrageous among the old cottages clustering nearby. In summer you can always find a weekend artist or two beavering away at Hutton Fellows. They love the view from the bottom of High Street, with the medieval bridge in the foreground.

"All right if you can afford the rates," said Rosher, who had just paid his and had it still fuming in his mind. He turned as the door began to open, arranging his features into the smile which, he was convinced, set the charm pulsating from him. If the more sensitive public tended to stiffen from shock when confronted with what looked like an ingratiating gorilla, they never mentioned it to him and he never noticed. That smile, and the telephone voice coupled with it, made of him, he believed, a living example to young policemen concerned with the fostering of good relations between police and public.

The door opened. A bald-headed man stood there. Not ill-looking even now, when the face was drawn and dark circles showed under the eyes. He'd have been about fifty, probably. Wore a good sweater, good slacks with a built-in crease and carpet slippers. He said: "Yes?"

Inspector Rosher, encased in his durable blue serge suit with double seat and the reinforced cuffs, the like of which is not made anymore, widened the smile, but not so far as was his wont when a ring on a door bell brought forth a lady. The full, brown-toothed beam he reserved for the female public, who also merited snatching off of the black hat and its gripping between hairy hands, in front of the barrel chest. This man was not female. The hat remained untouched and the telephone vowelling less mangled than it might have been as the inspector said: "Ah. Good morning, Mr. Poddy."

"Good morning," the man said. "Inspector . . . er . . . isn't it?"

"Rosher, sir. Yes." The last time he called it was to gather background information, to see if this man and his lady wife had any idea why their son should climb naked onto the roof of a low-grade rooming house, proclaiming himself the Son of God. The lad was by then in the psychiatric department of a hospital in the big city. Now, he was dead.

"Rosher. Yes. Er . . . come in." The man stood aside from the door.

"Thank you, sir." Now the black hat came off, as the inspec-

6

tor stepped into the scrubbed and polished hall followed by Sergeant Panton. A classic short-back-and-sides haircut stood splendidly forth, marred only by the tenpenny-piece-sized pink tonsure right up there on the crown.

The man led on over wall-to-wall carpet, into a drawing room that just missed elegance by reason of its lived-in look. Here was the lady of the house, ensconced in one of the big armchairs. "It's Inspector Rosher, dear," the husband told her. To tone with a middle-aged version of his son's good looks, he had a pleasant voice.

Now the beam attained full stature, the thick lips drew back from economy-size teeth that turned brown after German measles and never came back to the original Payne's Grey. Almost adenoidal in its mangling, the voice said: "Ah, Mrs. Poddy. Good morning, madam."

The lady was younger than her husband, perhaps in the mid-forties. To Rosher, she looked too young to have a son in his late teens. But then, so many people seemed so young, these days. He'd noticed it in policemen, and some of the parents you came across were hardly more than children. Even grandparents were much younger than they used to be. "Good morning, Inspector," the lady said quietly. Her eyes were red from recent weeping and she held a crumpled handkerchief, lace-edged.

"One is sorry to intrude upon you in this fashion," the inspector said. "One is here, of course, at the call of duty."

"It's quite all right," said the lady. "We expected you—or somebody—to call. Do sit down."

"Ah." The inspector beamed. And with what sympathy in it. "Thank you, you are very kind." He sat, in the armchair facing her across the width of the handsome stone fireplace. Mr. Poddy remained standing. So did the sergeant, who was observing Old Blubbergut's public manner with very great interest. This was the first time he had worked with the legendary Blubbergut, the man who got busted down and actually bounced up again. He'd heard the old bugger was a right comedian, but he was funnier than that. This house of grief was no place in which to feel the bubble of amusement rising in the belly, but you had to admit, it was very funny. Carefully, the sergeant kept his impassive face. "May one offer one's sincere condolences," the old gorilla said.

"Thank you," said both the parents; and the man added: "What can we do for you?"

"I have to ask you a few questions," said Inspector Rosher. "Purely routine, of course. You will understand that needs must, if we are to bring the miscreant to book."

Oh, thought young Sergeant Panton, did you ever! Needs must. Miscreant. Bring to book. A little snort escaped him. He turned it into a cough. Mr. Poddy said: "Of course, Inspector. We understand that."

"Thank you, sir. One was sure you would." The news was broken to them last night; but not by Rosher, who was still in the woodland clearing. As soon as he arrived, he had recognised the lad lying dead. Other policemen called here last night, other policemen took them in time to the morgue, to identify their son. No wonder their manner was subdued, their faces marked by stress. "Well, I believe your son was . . . er . . . came home a week ago." From the bug-hutch. The nuttery. But be tactful.

"That's right," said Mr. Poddy. "Yes."

"Can you think of anybody who might have disliked him? I mean—who would want to kill him?"

"Nobody." The word jerked out of Mrs. Poddy. She held the handkerchief against her quivering lips. "Why would anybody want to . . . to . . .?" Her husband stepped across, to lay a hand upon her shoulder; to squeeze it gently, comfortingly. She glanced up at him with great pain in her eyes. His encouraging smile was twisted with matching pain.

"Uh-huh. In the . . . er . . . hospital. He had been in before, I believe." I know. You told me yourself, when I was here before. "Could there have been, perhaps, a fellow-patient, anybody like that?" Because the psychiatric wards are filled with violents, and they release them every day. "Could he have made enemies or anything?"

Or anything? thought Sergeant Panton. Enemies or anything? But the tickle was moderating in his belly, overshadowed by the pain in this room. A sensitive young man—and it is surprising how many policemen are—he had not yet grown the extra skin a copper must have to shield himself against all the agony that comes his way. Either that, or resign, or go mad. One of the three he would do, in time.

"Did he have friends?"

Mr. Poddy answered. "Not many. His . . . condition . . . made it difficult. There was a lad called Tom. In hospital. I don't know his surname."

"It doesn't matter, sir." Other men were asking questions at the hospital. They would come back with names and addresses of anybody who knew the boy and mixed with him. "Anybody around here?"

"Not really. The twins. But they're his cousins, of course. And Fiona. That's about all. Isn't it, dear?" And Mrs. Poddy nodded, the lacy handkerchief twisting in her hands.

"Fiona?"

"Fiona Watson-Harvey. We'd hoped once . . . but of course it wasn't really . . . possible." Mr. Poddy stopped, to clear his throat. "But they remained friends."

"Well . . . at first. Though we do not use the word. When we came here two years ago. But he had one of his . . . times. And, of course, she couldn't be expected to. . . . But, yes, I think you could say she is . . . was . . . a friend."

"Can you give me her address, sir, please?"

"Yes. The Laurels. At the other end of the village."

"Next to my sister's place," Mrs. Poddy put in. "Big house, stands back from the road. You can't miss it."

"Thank you, madam." The inspector glanced sternly at Sergeant Panton, who immediately brought out his little black book to make the entry. "He was of a . . . er . . . religious nature? Your son?"

"We are Jehovah's Witnesses, Mr. Rosher," replied the man, quietly. "We told you, I believe, when you were here before."

"Uh-huh," said Rosher. It had explained a lot. "What I mean is . . . he embraced your . . . er . . . beliefs?"

For God's sake, the sergeant thought, why doesn't he just talk like a human being?

Mr. Poddy hesitated slightly. Then he said: "There was . . . difficulty . . . for a time. But he was coming to see—"

"He always saw." The mother cut in, sharply. "He never really strayed. Never." Her tear-reddened eyes met the inspector's, challengingly.

"Uh-huh," Rosher said again. "Were you aware that traces of drugs were found in the—in your son?" He'd almost said the body. Nobody ever called him a sensitive man, not even at his time of joining; but even he drew back from thrusting the word into their wounded faces.

Now both parents looked at him, eyes widened with shock. "Never. Never," Mr. Poddy said, jerking the word out. His wife picked it up.

"Never," she said.

For a moment there was silence. The inspector knew when to wait. Mr. Poddy made again that comforting squeeze at his wife's shoulder, that clearing of the throat before he spoke.

"They gave him . . . stuff . . . at the hospital. By no wish of ours, but we had no say in it, he was of age. Valium. It would have been . . . he would have had. . . ."

"Not Valium, sir, I am afraid. None of the drugs administered to combat his illness. We've checked. The hospital's told us what they supplied." And it wasn't cocaine, they didn't supply cocaine. Which he must have sniffed, because the only puncture marks in him the hospital people, called in to inspect, said they put there long ago, in rump and thigh.

It is normal for a mother, her son's rectitude attacked, to attack the attacker. Mrs. Poddy, stiffly upright in her big chair, glared now at the grim gorilla bulking on the other side of the fireplace. Her voice shrilled savagely as she said: "He never did— he never took drugs. Never. Not even the ones the hospital gave him . . . God's Will. . . ."

Shocked by the abrupt violence in her—he was very young.

10

Not without experience, but very young in cases of this gravity—Sergeant Panton thought: Christ—that's stirred it up a bit.

Mr. Poddy was squeezing his wife's shoulder again, saying in a soothing tone: "Easy, dear. Easy. Mr. Rosher is only doing what he must."

"That is correct, sir," said Rosher. He addressed Mrs. Poddy. "I am sorry, madam. Somebody killed your son. I have to examine every fact I can find. That's my duty."

Surprised again, the sergeant thought: dropped the cut-glass bit. Dignity. He suddenly got dignity. Wouldn't think he had it in him, would you?

Mrs. Poddy had put her hand over her husband's, as if to reassure him. Under control again, she said more quietly: "I am sorry, Mr. Rosher. It was . . . he didn't. He never would. Not Teddy. It was against all his . . . beliefs. Principles. He was . . . saved."

Saved? the sergeant thought. He was a bloody nut case. And, by the look of it, a junkie. And not long ago Old Blubbergut here stopped him flying off a roof. And he's been bloody murdered. What's so saved about that? Aye, aye—my old mate's getting up.

Inspector Rosher was indeed rising onto his bandy legs. He had picked up the black hat laid carefully upon the carpet where it would not be inadvertently crushed under his boxy-toed shoes and was holding it between those hairy hands, in front of his chest. A touch of the telephone mangling returned to his vowel sounds.

"Well, thank you very much, Mrs. Poddy. And you, sir. Again, my sincere condolences. I won't trouble you any more just now. Thank you for your cooperation."

"I'll see you out," Mr. Poddy said.

They left the scrupulous room and the front door bell sounded while the inspector was speaking, as they crossed the hall. He was saying: "Was he—I'm sorry to have to ask—ever violent?" Up on the roof he wasn't. Not until I grabbed him and the other buggers joined in.

"He was . . . a little . . . disturbed . . . once or twice."

"Uh-huh." Because I was wondering if he died in a fight.

Went for some young herbert with a knife in his sock. Scared the shit out of him, got himself done. Exit young herbert, running. "Well, thank you again, sir."

At the door Mr. Poddy turned aside to pick up a small booklet from an occasional table. "Perhaps this will interest you," he said. Then he opened the door.

Two good-looking young men stood under the porch, backlit by the remarkable sunshine and as like as two peas. Both in sports jacket and slacks, although these were different in pattern; both with good, brown curly hair and pleasantly snub-nosed faces. One of them said: "Hallo, Uncle Will. We just heard about Teddy. Hope it's not inconvenient—that's a police car—we can come back later." The policemen loomed. The young man finished: "Ah."

"No, no," said Mr. Poddy. "Come in. I'm afraid your Auntie is. . . . These are my wife's nephews, Mr. Rosher. Simon and Timothy."

"Howjedo," said Rosher.

"How do you do," the twins said; and the one who had not spoken before added: "Inspector Rosher. We saw you on television."

"You'd caught The Avenger," the other said. They picked each other's thinking up quickly, it was obvious. Twins, of course, often do. If they knew—and they should have, it was closer to home and in all the papers—that the inspector also brought their cousin down, and more recently, from a roof, neither of them mentioned it. Restrained, perhaps, by the presence of the cousin's father.

"Uh-huh," said Rosher. He had gathered a lot of kudos from his arrest of the maniac who called himself The Avenger, and a lot of publicity. Television, radio, newspapers. People remember. He was well used to being recognised. It's the telly that does it.

"Well, well," the first young man said; and added, as both turned their attention to Mr. Poddy: "We just got home, Uncle. Mother told us. It's—terrible. We just can't take it in. Who would. . . ?"

The policemen were through the door now. Mr. Poddy said,

with no very apparent enthusiasm: "Come in, boys." The two young men moved forward. Inspector Rosher settled the black hat low upon the brow; turned his bulk to say: "Good day, then, Mr. Poddy. Thank you once again for your help. We will keep you informed, of course." Of inquest date—of when you may bury your dead. Of this and that, whatever we think you ought to know.

"Good day, Mr. Rosher," said the father, and closed the door with his nephews inside, who looked out with interest at the serge-clad man so much bulkier and less affable than he seemed in glorious colour on a 24-inch screen. Same hat, though.

"I'll drive," the inspector said to Sergeant Panton; and when they were in the car he tossed Mr. Poddy's little booklet into the sergeant's lap, saying as he turned the ignition key: "That might do you a bit of good."

The sergeant glanced at the ill-printed cover. JESUS SAVES! the black type screamed. "I'm a Birmingham Buddhist, myself," he said.

3

Among all the false images foisted upon the public by cinema and television, radio and lady crime novelists of either sex, perhaps the most enduring is the police inspector—or chief inspector sometimes—plodding about all on his own, or with a constable written in so that he has somebody to help with the dialogue, handling murder cases without reference to anybody higher up. Aye, and solving them, too. If he be American, he will be called "Lootenant," and do it by leaping into a motor car and taking off in every direction with a skriek of burning tyres. Or tires. British or American, only the rank-title differs.

It does not happen that way, of course. It never did. A murder inquiry is a team effort, and the team can be a big one. At the outset it certainly will be, what with forensic men, fingerprint men, Scenes of Crime men, pathologists and everybody who knows Uncle Tom Cobleigh; but many of these specialists do not linger. Job done, they turn back to other matters, of which there are always plenty. But their going still leaves a team, of whom the inspector or inspectors is or are a relatively humble member or members, working under a Chief Superintendent, possibly a Superintendent or two, maybe a Chief Inspector. The exact composition of the team is not statutory, it varies according to available resources, complexity of the case, and various other factors. But from near or far, a Chief Constable will have his wary-parrot eye upon it. After all, he is the man who receives the ultimate can, in case of cockup.

When Inspector Rosher reached the station, he told Sergeant Panton to hang about, and to get on with some paperwork while he did so, because a policeman's book does not magically clear itself for murder, and if he finds himself spare for a time he does well to keep abreast of the paper accumulating around his other work. Once it snarls up it is one helluva job to get it straight again. And you don't like to hand over all your juicy morsels to other men, even when told to do so, as once you are on a murder case you probably will be. They'll only grab all the kudos, if they don't cock the lot up. So the young man inserted paper into the machine and flexed his two typing fingers quite willingly, at a desk in the C.I.D. room.

The inspector himself looked at the file of bumph that gathered about young Teddy Poddy at the time of capering on the roof. Many of the questions he might have asked this morning he had been able to skip. The answers were in here. He carried the file into his office, just along the corridor that thunks rather than clacks since they put the compo flooring down, and when he had hung up the black hat and battleship grey raincoat and smoothed his hair along the sides he rang through to let the Chief Constable know he was back and available. The Chief Constable said come up.

So Mr. Rosher took the file again in hand and went up the stairs to where the cokernut matting stopped at the door to the Chief's office. On the other side was good carpet, not bought off a market barrow. He knocked and was told to enter.

Three men were in the handsome office, where the biggest desk in the building proclaimed that here worked the biggest man. One was Chief Superintendent (Rollie) Rawlins, head of the uniform branch and here, not because he would be engaged in detection, but because his men were on house-to-house and all the routine foot-slog jobs that must be done. One was Detective Superintendent Archie Bishop, inevitably called the Archbishop and possessor, by design or the giggle of God, of a bland and avuncular

15

front to match. He could, when in form, string together clichés as fatuously as any real archbishop. It was said that when he gave a lecture at the police college, calling it Policing in Modern Britain, he had the whole room snoring in five and one half minutes. Mind you, they'd all been on the beer at lunch time. Very good detective, though. The third man was Detective Inspector Young Alec Cruse.

The Chief himself was at the window that commands an uninterrupted view of the station parking lot. No doubt he had been looking through it and seeing nothing, if he was pondering. Most people do this sort of thing. He had turned, and if he was speaking when the knock of knuckles came upon the door, had suspended it. He said as Rosher came in: "Ah, Mr. Rosher. You're back." Instantly abreast of both factors, without needing to think.

"Sir," said Rosher.

"Anything?"

"Not really." Rosher indicated his file. "We've got most of it in here."

"Good," the Chief said. "You've brought the file. Good. Splendid." A duplicate lay among the papers on his desk, as part of routine, but a note of encouraging approval never comes amiss. "I imagine the parents are taking it badly."

"Yes, sir. Very cut up."

"They would be. We were just sorting out what we have to work on. Sit down, sit down."

Rosher moved in to take the hard chair next to the one upon which sat Young Alec Cruse. Young Alec smiled his good smile and nodded. The Chief Constable took up his theme from where, presumably, he left it.

"So—we know the lad had a history of mental illness, dating back some years. We know he quite often left home for long periods, sleeping rough or in cheap rooming houses and so on. We know he came of religious stock and was subject to fits of religious mania, according to the hospital people. Well, we knew that anyway, from when Mr. Rosher distinguished himself in June. I believe he was undergoing some such fit then, Mr. Rosher?"

16

"Thought he was the Son of God, sir." It was all in the duplicate file, there on the desk. Rosher brought his own file, not because he thought it would be needed—he knew routine, if any man did—but because it is safest, if you have a file relating to a case, to bring it with you to top brass meetings. If you do need to check a point, you have it on your knee. Nobody has to ferret among the stuff on the top brass desk.

The Chief smiled benignly. He liked Rosher, being one of the few who did. Men invariably do take to their bosom the man who would not be here but for their just exercising of lawful authority. This was the man who snatched Rosher back from the reeking abyss above which the fierce and lion-headed (though spindly-legged) old Chief Constable, knife in hand to cut the rope, had him trussed and suspended. And all for a fumble at the mammalia of a publican's wife who in many years of teasing had enjoyed many a fumble, and come to no harm by it. So the new Chief smiled benignly as he said: "Meant to fly away, I believe?"

"That's what he said, sir, yes." The brownstone teeth glimmered. If the Chief wanted to share a beam, that was all right with Rosher. He was beholden to the man. If he secretly thought him a bit of a twat, he cannot be held responsible for the whisper of his essential nature. In some ways, he preferred the hard old bastard who'd bust him down and then set out to break him, without mercy. Rosher, who had done the same thing to ring opponents and many, many little bent fellow-humans, could respect that and hate the Old Man cleanly, stiffened against him. He didn't have to like him.

"Good job you were there," the Chief said; and then, realising that it hadn't done the lad such a very great favour, since he was dead now: "I mean—that would have been a nasty way to die." And then, realising that with a knife between the ribs is not the way many people would choose to end their days: "Mm. It was a good piece of work, anyway. Now: there were drugs in the body. Cocaine. No record of drug addiction, none whatever. One week out of hospital. Did he have any friends?"

Everybody looked at Rosher. "Only one known to his parents,

sir," the inspector said. "A lad called Tom, fellow inmate. Surname not known as yet—I shall get onto that as soon as we finish here." And being here at all is a bloody waste of time. "Two male cousins, twins, about his own age or a bit older. And a girl, a Miss Watson-Harvey. Fiona Watson-Harvey. Parents hoped she might marry him, but his habits—that is, his condition—put her off. Remained friends. Lives in village. Mother and father. Only child." All this reeled off without a note. Except to produce in court, your seasoned policeman seldom needs his book. Even its production there stems from the same principle that had Inspector Rosher sitting here with his file. It looks good, it helps to convince.

"Watson-Harvey," the Chief said. "I know some Watson-Harveys. Nice people. Did you see the girl?"

"No, sir. Called at the house on the way back." It was true, he did. Only the mother was in. "She was out. Riding. I asked them to get her to ring me when she comes in. Saw the two cousins, they were arriving as I left."

"At the Watson-Harvey's?"

"No, sir, at the Poddy's. To express condolences, as I understood it." Use of the singular reveals how much value the inspector put on his sergeant, bashing away with two fingers downstairs.

"Ah. Yes. Well: what it all amounts to is this. . . ."

Three, four minutes later, all the seated men got up and filed out, some of them having said hardly a word, certainly since Rosher arrived. From now on, when they met first thing every morning until the case was cleared for the Chief Constable's conference, they would have biscuits on a china plate and coffee in little fragile cups; but on this, the first morning of the inquiry, there had been no early meeting, people had been busy delegating other cases and gathering material relating to this. It was now almost lunchtime.

They all went down the stairs. The Archbishop said to Rosher in his episcopal manner: "I shall be in court this afternoon, Mr. Rosher. You know where to find me, if you need me. I would suggest that you concentrate on these people who knew him, the cousins and the young lady and what-not. The friend from the hospital may be useful."

No need for him to instruct the other men. The uniform boss would deploy his force as and where needed, juggling shifts and overtime to fit. Detective Inspector Cruse, known to one and all as Young Alec, had been assigned to oversee the HQ team, here at the station.

"Right," said Rosher, well satisfied; because Archie Bishop was no man's enemy. He'd hold the reins loosely, letting the nags do their own running and trusting them to run well. Oh, he'd whack them all right if they strayed; but he was no Percy Fillimore.

Chief Superintendent (Percy) Fillimore *was* the enemy. To Rosher. God, Who has His funny little ways, built into these two men the ultimate personality clash. Clapped upon the other, the eye of each grew red and stony, and the hackles rose. When the exigencies of the service forced them into working together, such was the fume between them that neither man—and both were good policemen, in their very different ways—gave of his best. Both knew it and blamed the other, which only exacerbated the condition.

But Percy was in Malaga, nursing his tender stomach on a late holiday and wishing to God, as did his wife, that they'd never come. Whereas Inspector Rosher was very glad they went. Had he known that Percy's holiday was being spent in his hotel bedroom, tottering to and fro with the Spanish Trots, he would have been gladder yet. As it was, he entered his office with good feelings. He would be working without Percy snuffing at his heels.

When Fiona Watson-Harvey came back from her ride she stabled her horse and took off his tackle; hung everything up in the smelly tack room and walked between the autumn flowerbeds, over the lawn, onto the path, and so to the house. The dog Rover, a big daft Doberman who rarely left her side, uncocked his leg beside an uncomplaining rosebush when he saw her go and lolloped with tongue lolling to catch her up. They came through the big front door together. Her mother's voice floated into the hall.

"Is that you, dear?"

"It's me, Mummy." A pretty girl after outdoor exercise looks her best, and provided she is slim-buttocked and high-breasted, jodhpurs and a canary-yellow sweater do nothing to lessen the effect.

"Did you have a nice ride?"

"Lovely. Through the woods and over the moors."

"Good. Come through, darling, will you? There is something I must tell you."

Here is another pleasant thing: nicely accented English female voices, calling mannerly to each other in a quiet old English house, built two centuries ago by a prosperous yeoman.

Girl and dog went through the hall and along the little passage leading to the kitchen, which was not as the yeoman's wife knew it. It had progressed from open fireplace and scrubbed oak through Victorian deal and black-leaded cooking range and all the subsequent adaptations until when the last yeoman left, eight years ago, the incoming Mrs. Watson-Harvey had the whole lot ripped out and bricking-up done. Cost a pretty penny; but she stood now among formica and all the electrical gadgets without which no home can be called a home, up to her elbows in flour and making a steak and kidney pie.

"What's up, Mumsy?" said Fiona. Not many girls call their mother Mumsy nowadays. It smacks of an age when young men in white popped in and out on Sundays, crying, "Anyone for tennis?"

Her mother, who had the same slim buttocks, big dark blue eyes and chestnut hair styled like a Botticelli angel, but was a touch less upstanding in the bust, looked at her gravely. "Darling," she said, "I don't want you to be upset. Please don't be upset. I know it's a terrible thing to say, but it may even be all for the best, poor boy."

"What might?" The dog Rover sniffed the air. Small blame to him, there was steak and kidney about.

20

"It's Teddy, dear. Teddy Poddy. I'm afraid he's . . . well . . . been murdered."

"Murdered?" The big blue eyes widened, the delicate mouth—and this, too, was very like her mother's—opened a little with shock. "Teddy? Good God."

"They found him—of course you will be upset. I am. Daddy was, when I rang to tell him—in Upshawe Wood. Apparently he had been stabbed."

"Good God," Fiona said again.

"Last night, from what I gather. His poor parents. I had a policeman earlier."

"Policeman?" said Fiona. "Who would . . . Teddy?"

"I know it's terrible," said her mother, "but—you mustn't be too upset, darling. The policeman wanted to speak to you. I said you were out."

"Me? Why me?" The blue eyes opened yet wider, huge in the fine-boned face. She really was a very pretty girl.

"He just wanted to ask you a few questions."

"Questions? What about?"

"Well . . . Teddy, I expect."

"I don't know anything about. . . . Why me?"

"I don't suppose it's only you, dear. I expect he'll be seeing everybody who knew poor Teddy. Your Daddy and me too, I expect, they do, I believe. Poor boy. I said you'd ring."

"Ring who?" A slim hand dropped to fondle the dog's ears; absently, as if to make sure he was there.

"The policeman, dear. At the town station. Ask for Roger."

"Roger?"

"That's what he said. Inspector Roger. Of course, things are much more informal nowadays. They probably use the Christian name to put people at ease; there's a lot about it on the television. Building a new relationship, it's all to do with the West Indians. Although, of course, there was that family in Stroud when I was a girl, their surname was Roger. I don't think it is all that uncom-

21

mon. And Rogers is common enough." Upset and shaken out of their routine, many women prattle.

"When am I supposed to ring?" Fiona asked.

"I said you'd do it when you came in. But I should have a cup of something first. Something hot and sweet. There's coffee ready, or I'll make you a cup of tea." Mrs. Watson-Harvey took up her packet of Goldie Bake Instant Mix and shook out a shower onto the dough she was kneading. Then she began to scrape it all off again. "Now look what I've done," she said. "Mind you, he wasn't really the type to put people at their ease. Most peculiar accent. And he looks extraordinarily like a gorilla."

Inspector Rosher did not stay long in his office. Lunchtime was here, for those who lunch early. Today, he would do that. I'll go now, he thought, while I've got the chance, and then if there's no sudden rush I'll get back to Hutton Fellows. The girl should have rung by then. I'll fix a time to have a word with her. And the two cousins—I'll have to ring Poddy, get their phone number. Don't know their name. And there's the matter of the nut-hutch friend—I'll get onto that now.

He reached for the telephone on his desk, and as he did so it rang. He picked it up and said, "Yes?"

"A young lady asking for you, Mr. Rosher," said the WPC on the switchboard. "I take it it's for you, she said Inspector Roger. A Miss Watson-Harvey."

"That's for me," said Rosher; and when the switchboard lass said go ahead, please: "Hallo."

"Inspector Roger?" came a clear, almost childish voice.

"Speaking." It was near enough. Russia—Rasher—Bosher—Basher—he'd been called them all, in his time.

"Oh. It's Fiona Watson-Harvey. My mother says you want to see me."

"I do, rather." The telephone voice was upon him, converting the I into Ai and rather into rawther. She was female public, with a very nice accent.

"What about?"

22

"I expect your mother told you that, miss." He could have been a playful uncle. The one a socially ambitious family would prefer to forget.

"She says it was about poor Teddy, she says he's been murdered."

"Perfectly correct, miss, yes. Unfortunately."

"Well—I don't know anything about it."

"No, of course not. Merely a matter of routine. We have to have a word with anybody who knew the victim, in a case like this. I was wondering if you will be at home after luncheon."

"I can be, yes."

"Ah. I shall be in your vicinity, quite adjacent. I wonder if I might call in."

"Well—yes. What time?"

"Shall we say two o'clock? Splendid. Goodbye, then, for now."

"Goodbye," said Fiona; and as she hung up, to her mother hovering in the background: "He's coming after lunch. I don't know why. I can't tell him anything."

"It's nothing to worry about, darling," said Mrs. Watson-Harvey. "You haven't done anything. What we need is another cup of tea." The dog Rover looked up at his adored young mistress with corrugated brow, bothered by her unease.

Rosher did not replace the phone. He kept it to his ear while he broke the connection with a finger, waggling the little bar to bring back the operator. When she came, he said: "Get me the hospital, will you? St. Joseph's. Psychiatric Department. Doctor Shultzburg."

A minute, and Doctor Shultzburg came on. He had a slight Continental accent and he was the psychiatrist who kept young Edward Poddy under his wing from June until a week ago. "Inspector Rozzer," he said. An original variation. "I was going to ring you. We had three Thomases here during Edward's time with us. Thomas Body, but he is seventy-two. Thomas Rance, he is forty and still with us. And Thomas Nolan, twenty-three. I think he will be the one you are thinking of. I believe he and Edward were together a lot. A good sign, when our people begin to emerge from isolation, that is a good sign. We encourage it."

"Do you still have him there?" the inspector asked.

"Only one morning a week, but he has missed the last two. He came to us in April and left in September, I have his file here. September the first. He has been attending once a week since, on Tuesday mornings, until two weeks ago."

"Uh-huh." Rosher was using his unadorned voice. The doctor's slight accent disqualified him from benefit of the cut-glass manner. Rosher had a poor opinion of foreigners and psychiatrists both. Dr. Shultzburg had the bad taste to be a foreign psychiatrist. "What was he in for?"

"He . . . er . . . where is it? Ah, here it is. He attacked a young woman. Under the influence of drugs. He had been indulging . . . yes . . . mm . . . caused a personality deterioration . . . indications of temporary paranoia. . . ."

"I'll just have the facts, doctor, if you please." I've had all the jargon before, I've heard your lot in the witness box. When it's not a lot of crap it's a load of bloody codswallop.

"Yes, yes, of course." Here is an aggressive personality, the doctor was thinking. Slight pathological tendencies assumed to cover a basic insecurity. "A man who came to her assistance sustained certain injuries. Mr. Nolan received a prison sentence suspended on condition that he underwent in-patient treatment."

"And you let him out again."

The doctor had a personality prone to huffiness. He knew it, he knew the childhood insecurities from which it sprang, he even knew that his physical characteristics (short and fat) may or may not—research has not yet decided—have contributed to it. But he couldn't help it. He said rather stiffly: "We do not keep people here forever, Mr. Rozzer. We are not a prison."

"Where does he live?"

"In various lodgings. No fixed address, when he came to us. Our social workers obtained a room for him when he left. Thirty-

24

four Enright Gardens. That's in Belton." Belton is a suburb of the big city. Not very far from the hospital.

"Thank you, doctor. We may have to call upon you again."

"You're welcome," the doctor said.

Rosher put the phone down and selected a button on his intercom. The voice of Young Alec Cruse spoke out plainly. "Yes."

The inspector did not give his name. Stiff awkwardness lingered still between these two men, dating from when Young Alec, then the detective sergeant assisting him on a murder investigation, had been called to witness against him at the official enquiry that resulted in Rosher's busting down to sergeant. Soon after, the young man found himself promoted to fill the resultant establishment gap and awarded Rosher's old office, that man now toiling away at a sergeant's desk. Even Rosher's re-elevation could not remove Cruse's feeling that the first event bore upon the second. Rarely could either bring himself to address the other by name, and never by rank. So Rosher said, brusquely: "There's a nutter. Thomas Nolan, they let him out of the hutch in September. Hasn't been in for two weeks, supposed to go every week. Said to be matey with young Poddy. History of violence—check with the city, he may be in breach of a suspended. Think we ought to sort him out."

Cruse knew who was speaking. For one thing, who having heard Rosher once would not know him when he came again? For another: anybody else would have said Alec, this is George. Or Harry, or Fred. "Right," he said. "Where could we find him?"

"No fixed. Should be living at—" The inspector filled in what details he had, knowing that they were being scribbled down at the other end. Then he clicked his little switch without farewell and went up to the canteen. It was Sausage Toad day. Caramel Custard to follow.

4

When Inspector Rosher had washed down his meal with two cups of the bitter black tea which they know so well how to produce in police canteens, he went down to the C.I.D. room where Detective Sergeant Panton was still tapping away at one of the desks, stuck his head through the door and said: "Get your hat, lad. We're off to Hutton Fellows."

"Ah," said the sergeant, "I . . . er . . . haven't had lunch yet." He was one who preferred a late lunch. It added to the pleasure, putting it off until he was really hungry.

"Should know better by now. Grab it while you can get it. Better bring a sandwich, eat it in the car. Five minutes, on the forecourt."

Five minutes later the young man peeled the plastic from an egg and cress sandwich—the canteen lady grows the cress herself, in boxes on the window sill. Subtracts a percentage from the price of the sandwich. Nobody minds, every trade has its perks—and bit into it as Rosher let in the clutch and took the car out into the town streets. Long before they were clear of the shopping centre the last steamed crumb was gone and he was working on the ham. By the time they reached the traffic lights where you turn onto the Hutton Fellows road (it is not very far) he sat empty handed with stomach growling, wishing he'd added a cheese with piccallily and perhaps an Individual Fruit Pie.

They travelled in Rosher's own car. A certain profit accrues from the petrol-plus-wear-and-tear allowance to the man who knows how to garner it. Rosher knew how, and was never one to pass over profit. The car was due soon for its annual M.O.T. examination, and the man who fears he has worn trunnions needs all the help he can get.

The country spread around the town is very lovely, nowhere lovelier than out toward Hutton Fellows; and far beyond, right up to the distressing purlieus of the big city. In this unseasonable October it was at its glorious best, unless you prefer the spring. All the wooded hills glowed richly, all the reaped fields were gold. The bracken, the heather were magnificent this year, having fed all summer on rain, and the farms stood washed and peaceful, sunshine come at last to ease the rheumaticky brick. Sheep and cows munched happily in green pastures untroubled by thought of the coming abatoir and all the distances were soft with a blue mistiness that comes only with autumn, and that about one year in ten.

To Rosher, all this glory meant nothing. See one tree, you've seen 'em all. The town was his and glory was long ago, when he stood in the boxing ring with the flame of it fierce in his heart as he danced begloved and bandy on jigging feet, knowing the bastard recently clobbered with the Mighty Hammer and now lying on the floor wasn't going to get up for quite some time. Glory stood on the sideboard now, cups and shields and medals gathering dust.

Nevertheless, within that simian frame dwelt a human spirit, and the human spirit expands willy-nilly in England under the benign caress of an unexpected sun. There was also, of course, the fact that Percy Fillimore was out of the way. He felt within him a rare joviality. So much so that when a rumble sounded above the engine note, he said cheerfully: "What's that?"

"What's what?" asked Sergeant Panton.

"That growling noise."

"My stomach."

"Ah. Well, don't do it, lad, there's a good boy. Had me worried. Thought there was something wrong with the car." Came a glimmer of the brownstone teeth, to announce the condescension of a joke.

Of all that was pretty today, nothing stood prettier under the wide blue sky than the village itself, its one main street, once you are over the bridge, lined with thatched or tiled cottages set back in gardens behind the row of horse chestnut trees. Gardens and trees flamed now in their dying riot and the ivy trained over the aged inn, sadly tarted for tourists but the main structure much as it was when men drank here from leather mugs, blared Walt Disney technicolour. Dwarfs could have marched out of it, whistling while they worked. Rosher drove through this happy street and on for a mile beyond, back to the house where he'd called briefly this morning after seeing the murdered youth's parents.

He stood again with Sergeant Panton under the porch set about with potted plants, and pressed the bell. It was answered this time by a very pretty blue-eyed girl who had changed out of jodhpurs into jeans but still wore the canary-yellow sweater. Had she donned a frillyish chiffon dress and a floppy hat she would have been the perfect English rose. As it was, Sergeant Panton noted the out-thrusting breasts with approval.

But Inspector Rosher was done with such things, traumatised into impotence. Only a brothel madam and a West Indian nurse had stirred it since his libido-engendered disaster. He snatched off the black hat and held it between both hands in front of his chest; bared the great teeth and said winningly: "Ah, good afternoon. Miss Watson-Harvey?" Except that it acknowledged her feminine status, none of this had anything to do with sex.

"Yes," the girl said. "Inspector Roger?"

"Rosher, miss, ectually." The inspector held out his ID card in its long-matured little wallet.

"Ah. Come in." The girl stood aside. The policemen entered. A lady as beautiful in an older way as the younger came down a lovely curved stairway into the lovely hall. "Ah, Inspector Roger," she cried, beaming. "Back again? I see you have met my daughter."

The inspector beamed back at her, stripping the brownstone teeth to the very gum. "Indeed Ai hev, medem, yers," he said.

Here we go again, thought Sergeant Panton.

"The drawing room I think, dear, don't you?" said Mrs. Watson-Harvey, turning a beam as toothy (but of course, very much whiter) on her daughter. And they all trooped into one of those drawing rooms most usually seen in Ideal Homes. Indeed, copies of it lay on the low table between fine settee and matching chairs in front of the impressive fireplace. Oh yes, there had been changes made since the yeomen were here. "Sit down, do," the lady said. "We will sit on the settee, Fiona. Side by side, like two of the brass monkeys. Moral support, eh, dear?" she twinkled at her daughter.

"Oh, Mumsy," said Fiona. "For God's sake!" Even pouting she was pretty.

Rosher sat down, placing the black hat carefully on the carpet beside the chair. No need for him to remain standing to establish psychological advantage, it was not that kind of interview. Sergeant Panton sat down, bringing out his little notebook. The inspector said: "Well, now, I shan't bother you long, Miss Watson-Harvey. I merely wondered if you know of any . . . er . . . body who might have wanted to harm Mr. Poddy junior."

As he spoke he did the thing that those who knew him best dreaded most. He drew out a great handkerchief, degenerated into crumpled greyness since the days when the fat wife, gone home long ago to Mother, sent him forth each day with linen whiter than white; and lifting it to his wide nostrils, he blew.

Only the knowledgeable sergeant was braced. The two unversed ladies started like ponies walloped suddenly upon the withers, matching blue eyes widened with shock. Fiona's soft mouth moved to make a little o. Her mother's social beam tugged itself sideways and she shot a glance at the cabinet holding her most fragile china. Shut in the kitchen, the dog Rover erupted madly. When the Rosher-echo died, Mrs. Watson-Harvey said: "What was the question again? BE QUIET, ROVER!!"

The dog subsided to a mix of bark and growling. Inspector Rosher commenced his mopping-up ritual. He wiped; restored the handkerchief to the pocket of his durable blue serge trousers; coughed, and while he repeated the question raised one thick forefinger to scratch delicately the little pink tonsure on his crown. Alone, or among familiars, he tended to finish the routine with a thoughtful scratch at a buttock, but never with ladies present.

No, Fiona said, she did not know of anybody who would wish to harm Teddy. No, she did not know any of his friends. If he had any—he kept very much to himself. Well, she wouldn't say (nor would her mother, who murmured and shook her head so to signify) that she was ever his girlfriend. Not really. She went around with him a good deal—oh, about a year ago—but that was before she realised he was . . . well . . . ill. It didn't always show, for long periods he was, you know, quite normal. He could be very . . . charming. When he was . . . well . . . normal.

All very routine, and over in a few minutes with nothing entered in the sergeant's little book. He only took it out to note any names and addresses supplied. When the inspector reached down for the hat, back it went into his pocket, little pencil tucked in neatly under the spine. Rosher said as he rose, jovial as the Santa Claus who comes to young monkeys deep in the jungle on Christmas Eve, provided they have been good: "Well, thank you, miss, for your cooperation. And you, madam. Forgive us for taking up your valuable time, we have to do these things. A sad business, very."

"Indeed it is," said Mrs. Watson-Harvey. The dog was growling still. "Would you care for coffee before you go?"

"Thank you, Madam, no." Hat clutched before his chest, the inspector stood beaming appreciation of the offer.

"Tea?"

"No thank you, I have other calls to make. Most kind. I expect you know the two boys, Mr. Poddy's cousins."

"Yes, of course. Simon and Timothy."

"Which is their house, exactly?" He'd forgotten to find out, but it did not matter. Everybody in a village knows everybody.

"The big Georgian farmhouse. Just before you reach the village. You can't miss it—next house to this, actually."

"Thank you. We'll be away, then."

"Will you see the gentlemen off, Fiona darling?" said Mrs.

Watson-Harvey. "I'll let Rover out of the kitchen, before he has the door down."

Out of the house and under the porch, the inspector did another of his own things. He donned his black hat and immediately snatched it off again, to beam at the girl standing in the doorway. "Thank you once more, Miss Watson-Harvey," he said. "We won't be bothering you again. Good afternoon."

"Good afternoon," said Fiona, and shut the door as Rover rushed into the hall, growling still.

The two policemen walked toward the car left in the drive. The sergeant said: "Bloody big dog. Helluva growl on him."

Jovial still, Inspector Rosher replied: "Wonder you could hear him, the row your belly was making. You'll have to learn how to conduct yourself in front of the public, lad. I was quite ashamed of you." He bandied on. You have to hand it to him, the sergeant thought: he's very, very thick.

Before the car engine started, Fiona was up the stairs with the big dog padding alongside, slobbering his relief at having her back at his altar where she belonged. Up in her Ideal Homes bedroom she picked up the yellow-and-buff Fanciphone and dialled the number; saying when the earpiece spoke: "Simon?"

"Timothy," the voice said. Physically and vocally it was hard to tell which was which. On phones, you simply advanced one name, receiving clarification more speedily than if you said who's speaking, please.

"Ah. There's an Inspector Rosher just been. He's on the way to see you."

The voice in the earpiece took on amusement. "So? What have we got to be afraid of?"

"About Teddy."

"Ah yes. Poor old Teddy."

"Just thought I'd let you know."

"Lovely of you, sweetheart. Anything else?"

"No. I just thought I'd let you know."

"See you, then. Look after yourself."

"Tim . . . you didn't. . . ?"

"At a time like this? Don't be silly, dear." A click, and he was gone. Fiona and dog went swiftly down the stairs.

Her mother, having attained the kitchen, had stayed in it. She was brewing tea, which she kept in a beautifully laquered caddy. That didn't come with 4p off from a supermarket. Nor did the tea. She said: "Did you go upstairs, dear?"

"Only to wee-wee, Mumsy."

"Why didn't you use the one downstairs?"

"I needed a hankie, too."

"Not catching a cold, darling, are we? I do hope we're not catching a little cold."

"Oh, Mumsy, don't fuss."

"Mumsy loves you, darling, that's all. You look quite pale. I know what you need—a nice hot cup of tea. I say, did you ever hear anything like it?"

"Like what?"

"When he blew his nose. He ought to hire himself out to factories. I *said* he was like a gorilla, didn't I? Extraordinary man. And what an odd voice, do you think he needs his adenoids removed? He didn't upset you, dear, did he?"

"Oh, Mother. Why should I be upset?"

"I think you are, though, just a teensy-weensy bit. It's the shock, I expect, and then the naughty man coming and making you talk about it. Mumsy can tell, when her little girl is upset."

"Oh, for God's sake, Mother," said Fiona.

The house where the twins lived was yet another old farm, and this one used still in some measure for farming, as was clear from the outhouses and the sheep in the meadow behind. It stood four-square and solid, the original facade spoiled by Victorian improvement, back from the main road beyond a front garden heavy with holly and yew trees, much less cared for than most of the gardens hereabout. Inside, the furniture was heavy and inelegant. Detective Inspector Rosher sat among it saying to the two young men and a lady without clothes sense: "I am sorry to put you to this inconvenience. Needs must, I am afraid."

"Quite all right, Inspector," one of the twins replied. It was Simon, wearing a blue waterproof jacket with jeans and well-used boots.

"Quite an honour to have you visit us," said Timothy. He was dressed in tweed. Jacket and trousers, with the same heavy footwear. "We've seen you on telly, several times."

"Uh-huh." The inspector was not ill-pleased, because policemen are human. They enjoy deferential reference to their peaks of achievement as much as the next man. He made his joke, even. Not a man given to levity, but he knew all the proper rejoinders. "I trust it didn't break the set."

Everybody smiled politely, the boys with a white showing of strong young teeth, the lady with a nervous glimmer of expensive ones, very brief as if she knew she should not be doing it. Even the sergeant smiled. It was his duty. The public faced with two policemen must not be given hint that the junior thinks the senior a right old twat.

"We merely wondered," the inspector said when the smiling was over and done, "whether you can help us in any way in our inquiry into the sad demise of Mr. Poddy junior." When he had his telephone voice on, his verbal style leaned to the archaic and long-winded. Undertakers lean the same way, and they, too, wear black hats.

"In what way, Inspector?" Simon asked.

"You are Mr.—?" Eyebrows like untrimmed privet hedges rose enquiringly.

The young man looked surprised. "Wellington," he said; and then, smiling again, he pointed to his smiling brother. "He's Timothy. I'm Simon."

Again the brownstone teeth shone forth. "Not easy for a stranger to tell you apart. No doubt your mother can." The teeth turned in the direction of the lady, sitting on an uncomfortable leather chair. All the chairs were uncomfortable.

"Yes," the lady said. Almost the first words she had spoken. A quiet, ravaged-looking person, and one with her hair coming down.

Rosher turned back to the twins. "You would have known Mr. Poddy well, of course?"

"Of course," said Simon.

"He was our cousin," said Timothy.

"Not that we were ever boon companions," said Simon.

"Not really, no," said Timothy.

"Ah," said Inspector Rosher. "Can you think of anybody who might desire his death?"

"No. Nobody." This was Simon.

"Nobody. No." That was Timothy.

And so the interview went, all the same questions asked over again; as in cases where the victim has a wide circle of friends and relatives, they are asked over and over and over again. Very little glamour in police work. This is the way it is done. Ninety-nine percent of it fruitless. The trick is, to spot fruit in the other one percent.

It didn't seem to be here. The lads appeared to know not much more about their cousin than young Fiona did, except that he had been subject to bouts of enthusiastic religion as far back as they remembered him. He came, as they pointed out, from very religious parents. The inspector gathered that if religion ran in the family it had skipped this sister, the quiet lady with the falling hair. Probably Mrs. Poddy caught it from her husband. It often happens. And child enthusiasm, of course, is commonly donned to win parental approval. He got up to go. The sergeant got up. The twins got up; all from leather chairs stuffed, by the feel of it, with hair from a very tough horse. Mrs. Wellington remained seated.

"Good afternoon, then, madam," said Rosher; and inevitably: "Thank you for your cooperation."

"Good afternoon," the lady murmured. Her eyes were light blue, watery as weak eyes often are. Really, she did not look at all well.

"We'll see you out," said Simon.

The hall shared the rather glum heaviness of the room they had left; cumbersome chairs and tables standing about, an awkward-looking brown-varnished coatrack and thick, bulbous bannisters to the stairs. No flowers in vases, just one glooming rubber plant in a brown urn. Inspector Rosher turned at the door to deliver his usual parting word.

"Thank you once again, gentlemen, for giving up your valuable time."

One of the twins—and what does it matter which? They were virtually interchangeable—said: "Just hope you catch whoever did it."

The other said: "Yes, indeed."

"We shall, sir, never fear." Sharp little eyes glancing around at the indications, the inspector added: "Keep the place going as a farm, do you?"

"Not really," said Simon. "We don't grow crops."

"Sheep," said Timothy. "Southdowns. We're crossing them with Suffolks."

"Hope it's profitable."

"Not bad. It'll be better when we have a sideboard full of prizes." It was difficult, unless you were watching closely, to tell who was saying what.

"Best of luck, then. Like a bit of roast lamb myself. Good afternoon." Away went the bandy legs, carrying the ape-man body to the car. Sergeant Panton nodded farewell and followed after.

The two young men shut the door and let their faces relax into broad grins, laughter bubbling up when they looked at each other. "What a character," said Simon. "He couldn't catch pussy unless it climbed a tree."

"That's where he belongs. Wonder how he nobbled that Avenger chap?" It's true: the public school educated still call people chaps. "I say, you chaps," they cry. Even at Girton.

"Just got lucky. And the fellow was a nutter, not very clever."

The degree of mental rapport between twins really is amazing. Simultaneously as they walked from the door back to that heavy room, they rounded their shoulders to let the arms hang down, pushed the tongue forward to bulge the area beneath the lower lip, stuck their backsides out and walked very bandy. They even scratched under their arms from time to time, the piss-taking young rips. Right into the room they went like this; but to amuse themselves only. Not their mother, who was still sitting there. Poor lady, she was seldom amused.

By now the short October day was closing down toward dusk, the setting sun throwing long sideways shadows and autumn nip coming into the air. It would be dark in an hour, with no moon; and soon after, the dog Rover would be out, all on his own.

5

Fiona looked more than usually pretty this evening. She knew well the art of makeup and she had inherited from her mother, or learned it by example, the sort of Harper's Bazaar dress-sense that goes with an Ideal Homes environment.

They were not without money, these Watson-Harveys. Daddy inherited the family tea-importing business from his father (said to have died from a surfeit of tannin) and he was proud of his pretty women. Particularly, of his daughter. So the women, with no need to earn a living (Mrs. Watson-Harvey could have had servants and a cook if she'd wanted them—but she didn't), spend a good deal of time discussing clothes and shopping for them and, as often as not, altering what they had bought to exactly what they visualised when they set out hunting.

So tonight Fiona came down the stairs wearing black velvet slacks so tight as to cling between delicate buttocks and to prove beyond reasonable doubt her gender when viewed from the front, with a silver-white top quite loose, but artfully constructed to emphasise the breasts. And why not, for God's sake? They don't stay that shape for long. Her chestnut hair sparkled, freshly washed and lacquered, set off by pearl earrings in pink, small ears. Rover beside her, she tripped in high-heeled dancing shoes through the hall and into the living room, where her parents sat in the two lovely chairs that had held rugged policemen, earlier in the day.

Both parents looked up; her father from work brought home

with him, for a man must labour above the ordinary to support two pretty women in the style they graciously accept; her mother from an embroidered table cloth destined for a stall at the next Ladies Guild Sale of Work. "All right, darling," Mrs. Watson-Harvey said. "Don't be *too* late, will you? My, you *do* look pretty. It was a good idea, altering that neckline. Doesn't she look pretty, Daddy?"

"Indeed she does," said Mr. Watson-Harvey. A trifle abstracted, perhaps, but still by long habit injecting it with a touch of tolerant baby-talk. Even more than mothers, fathers find it difficult to see a loved daughter as grown-up. If eighteen can be said to be grown-up. "Be a few more hearts broken tonight, eh? Eh?"

"Don't be silly, Daddy," Fiona said. "Come on, Rover. Come on, silly—the kitchen."

The dog went reluctantly, tail down and eyes pleading, making a little whine; knowing that she was taking the love out of his life, that she was deserting him. Tonight she shut him away, he and his breaking heart, without a kiss, without so much as a hug. Not in these clothes, with hair and makeup freshly done. A dog's frantic tongue works havoc. And less than half an hour ago, with teasing enjoyment, she had encouraged the liberties dogs like to take, in bedrooms where the adored mistress stands before the mirror naked. It stirred her for the evening; and the stirred girl feels good, looks good and has most fun at dances. Not that she expected tonight to be rich in fun. Too much on her mind.

"Have you got everything, dear?" said Mrs. Watson-Harvey as she was being kissed. "Handkerchief? Money in case you have to get a taxi home?"

"Oh, Mumsy—the boys are bringing me home."

"*Only* if they haven't had a drink. I will *not* have you getting into that car if they've been drinking."

"Mumsy, they hardly drink, you know that."

By now, her father was receiving his kiss on the head. The very upper forehead, just forward of the hair trained over to disguise a receding hairline. He put his word in. "Your mummy's right, Chick-chick. You never know who *is* drinking, young people nowadays." A bit jumbled, but he knew what he meant.

"Silly Daddy," Fiona said, and gave him a bonus kiss. "As if I'd get into a car with anybody who'd been drinking."

"There's a good girl." He patted her fondly; but nowhere intimate, and careful to avoid the hair. He learned it long ago, from she and her mother both: never disturb the hair. "Have a good time."

"Just see that you don't," said Mrs. Watson-Harvey, forbidding the car, not the good time. She rose and went to see her daughter off, with another wee kiss on the doormat.

Shrouded at the vulnerable top with her cashmere shawl—one of them—Fiona walked down the drive as she did every week, and had done for some months past. Gentlemen would have come to pick her up, and her parents had told her so; but she said, "Good God—it's not the Dark Ages." The twins, if anybody was, were resposible for her itching sexuality. They felt no need to act like gentlemen. But they always drove her home.

Her mother, back in the lovely drawing room, said to the father: "I really cannot see why they go to that place all the time."

"The done thing, I expect," he replied, absently with his eyes down to his paperwork. "You know what young people are."

"But it's such a *dull* place, the town. No *real* entertainment—no really decent shops, even."

"She doesn't go shopping, dear. She goes dancing. I don't suppose it's dull when you're dancing."

The mother was not listening. Pretty women seldom do, to their hard-working, half-bald husbands. They use them, when they are there, mostly as sounding-boards against which to speak thoughts aloud. "She doesn't like the town, she often says so. You'd think she'd go to the city, there's plenty going on there."

"Perhaps the boys prefer the town. She goes with the boys." Seventeen hundred pounds, take away two is sixteen hundred and ninety-eight . . . keep your mind on your figures.

"If the boys had any gentlemanly feelings, they'd go where *she* wants to go."

"Uh-huh," said Mr. Watson-Harvey. He long ago gave up trying to follow his wife's mental leapings, even when he was in better form. "Perhaps she wants to go to the town, dear. . . and twelve is seventeen hundred and ten. . . ."

"Oh, George—that's no excuse, and you know it. They should *ask* her where *she* would like to go."

"Uh-huh." Add the ten percent, equals seventeen hundred and seventy-one—plus eight hundred and sixty-nine pounds, fifty eight pee. . . .

Fiona was going, as she always did unless the way was muddy, when she drove her little car down, out of the drive, along the road and round by the cinder path skirting the field at the back of the Wellington house. It brought her to the back door, which used to be the front door when the yard into which it opened was the true focal point of the farm. But times change, and the main porch, the letter box, the brass bell are all on the garden side now, put there by weird Victorians.

The original back facade has changed, too, with the door moved further along to make space for French windows. When she got to them she tapped on the glass, turned the handle and went straight in.

The twins were here, both dressed in well-cut jeans and leather jackets; Simon combing his hair at the mirror above the sideboard, Timothy easing his feet into shoes. He said as she entered: "Ah—there she is. The thinking man's instant erection."

She came at once to the critical point. "I don't think we should go tonight."

Simon was giving his hair the last securing pat. He pocketed his comb, grinning at her. "Don't you, duckie? Why's that?"

"I should think you'd know why."

Timothy, too, was grinning. He stood up. "Why should we know why?"

"Don't play games. That bloody policeman—"

40

"Old Monkeyman? What's he got to do with it?"

"He was here, wasn't he? And at my place."

"Routine," Timothy said. "Asking about Teddy. Nothing to do with us."

"Isn't it?"

"Of course it isn't. Do you think we did it? Don't be bloody daft. We haven't even seen him since he came out. Have you?"

"I—we ought to stay away tonight."

"The mail must go through," intoned Simon, dramatically. He moved to where she stood, slipped one arm around her, to cup and gently knead a breast. "Getting up-tight, are we? Need a little something, to quieten us down?"

"Haven't got time, have we?" said Timothy. "Unless we do it in the back seat while you drive, on the way down."

"Leave me alone," Fiona said. She covered the kneading hand with hers, making to pull it away but the grins broadened on the so-alike faces. They knew, these lads, that she wouldn't do it. Couldn't do it—never had been able to since they, three years the elder, introduced her to the art and craft when she was eleven. Mind you, she was more than willing.

It was Simon who did the releasing. One last, teasing squeeze that drew a small gasp from her and he let go of the pretty, yielding thing, took his arm away and crossed to the table, where two oblong packages lay, one small and one the size of a boot box. "Catch," he said, tossing the smaller one to her. "Right. Are we ready, then?"

"I still don't think we should go," said Fiona, the package in her hands. "It's too—close."

Timothy spoke. "No, no, no. Nothing to worry about at all. They always do that, when somebody's murdered. They interview all his friends and so on. Bound to, aren't they? So think of all the little people, twitching if they don't get their little jabs and sniffs." And think of the money. The necessary cash-flow.

"Sod the little people," said Fiona. "I wish I was out of it."

The grin left Simon's face. "But you're not, duckie, are you? So gird up your knickers."

They went out to the car and drove away, Fiona with the small package in her handbag, Timothy holding the other in his lap. Had she been a brighter girl, she would have known that two different cargoes were being carried. Drugs do not normally travel in parcels so large as the bigger one, and the bigger ones that came with them on every trip. But she was born for beauty, not for brightness.

As for the boys: call it, if you will, arrogant overconfidence. They had no fear at all. Never even considered not going, with money waiting and the financial situation poised as it was.

There was nothing doing at all, in the case of the murder of Teddy Poddy. There were no obvious clues, no leads. No knife, with or without gorgeous fingerprints all along the smooth bone handle that fingerprint men love, as they love liquor glasses and mirrors and of course windows, when these have been left ajar where the burglars went through.

Inspector Young Alec Cruse had men calling and inquiries going on all over the place, but none had as yet unearthed Tom Nolan. A general call was out now, to all police forces everywhere: pick him up if you can. Trouble was, nobody had a photograph of him to put on the wire machine. He lived alone in various cheap rooms and dosshouses, and when he had no money at all he slept rough.

Now there is nothing unusual about all this. The dead spell is common at the front end of a murder hunt. The Chief Constable said, at about the time when Fiona left her nice home: "Well, Mr. Bishop, what do you think?"

"Not much point in hanging around, sir," the Archbishop intoned.

"That's what I was thinking. Better get what rest you can, before things begin to hum."

This is routine police procedure, based on good, experienced commonsense. A fresh, well-rested policeman will cope comfortably, even if the case, when it breaks, keeps him from more than a cat-nap in a chair for days and nights on end. One made weary beforehand can commit mistakes. What goes for one goes for all, so some of the men who would be called upon were off duty already, their telephone numbers pinned up at the switchboard. Sergeant Panton, for one, was gone. Inspector Cruse was working, because he had all these men out. Inspector Rosher could have been away but was here still, having nowhere better to go.

"Right, sir," said Archie Bishop. "We're having Chicken Supreme, I believe. I'll ring the wife, tell her I'm on the way."

"Very nice, too," the Chief said. He was smiling. He liked a little levity in his dealings with his men, especially senior officers. Provided it did not go too far. A happy force is an efficient force, he always said. Snide men whispered that this one was no more efficient now than under that fierce old bastard, his predecessor. "Will you be leaving somebody on?"

"I'll stay, sir," said Rosher. There was a room here where camp beds were run in for officers who needed to be on immediate hand.

"Not necessary," the Archbishop pontificated. "Inspector Fardon is on nights." A phone call or two, and the whole team would come running. Most of them would even have shaved, overnight or on the way.

"Uh-huh," said Rosher. Not pleased, not displeased. He would sooner stay here than go home to his cluttered, chilly and unloved house on the hill, but it was a minor matter. Archie Bishop was right: the full cover of the night shift made it unnecessary for anybody to stay.

"I'll see you in the morning, then." The Chief smiled benevolently upon them both. The more so upon the inspector because he was working nicely, riding tandem with Archie Bishop. And he could work nicely, very nicely, provided that he was not furiously pedalling one way while Detective Chief Superintendent (Percy) Fillimore as furiously pedalled another. For once, there was no danger of their colliding.

"You will be joining me for coffee in the morning?" This was the Chief's way of reminding them that he would expect them in his office first thing tomorrow. No need to remind them, but he was a man of courtesy.

"Thank you, sir," said Superintendent Bishop. Rosher said much the same.

"Goodnight, then, gentlemen." And the Chief went home.

Not long after, the Archbishop also left. Rosher stayed for awhile. He was not a drinking man, the pubs and clubs knew him only when he used them as gathering-ground for information and to keep an eye on what the little bent were up to. He belonged to no social fraternity, he had no friends and no hot supper awaited him. He had beans and bacon in the fridge, fat congealed on the cooker and a pile of unwashed crockery in the sink. So he ate cod and chips in the upstairs canteen, lingered over his bitter tea, and left the station at just about the time when Mr. Watson-Harvey spoke to his wife.

He said: "It's no use, dear. I simply cannot concentrate with Rover doing that."

The dog was whining continuously, putting in a bark now and again. He always did when his beloved left him, and nobody really minded. He should have been let out by now, to roam about and be fussed as necessary in the drawing room, because the whole family was fond of him; but tonight, Daddy was working.

"Shall I let him out?" his wife asked.

When she said out, she did not mean into the night. Nor into here. Physically present, he demanded physical attention, which would compound the current problem; and if they opened the back door to give him the run of the garden, he'd be over the gate in a flash, gone seeking Fiona. But on occasions like this, or when friends were in for bridge, he often went into the stable with Rock-abilly (called Rockie) the horse. He liked Rockie and found comfort in his company, partly perhaps because traces of the scent of the girl who rode him clung about him.

"I'll do it, dear," said Mr. Watson-Harvey. There was never any doubt that he would. For one thing, in his dealings with his pretty women he was nothing if not a gentleman. For another, a

44

Doberman on a lead can pull a smallish woman flat on her face, or, if the leash snags, whirl her over the gate and away like a frantic kite in a half gale. So Mrs. Watson-Harvey settled back and got on with her tatting.

Mr. Watson-Harvey put his work carefully on one side and his spectacles on top. He got up; went into the kitchen, where the lead hung; said: "Come on, lad—let's go and see Rockie." A minute later Rover was tugging sideways and whining as they crossed the yard, and Mr. Watson-Harvey, braced and tugging in opposition, was snarling: "Come here, you daft bastard. Come *here*, you sod." Because his women were not here, and he could say what he liked. Could jerk the lead as hard as he liked, too.

In the dark stable the horse, bored and with nothing to do having already thrown all his feed out of the manger, fixed them with mournful eyes when the light went on. Time not out galloping hangs heavy for a gelding, who cannot even pass it in dreams of fair fillies without weeping for what might have been. Mr. Watson-Harvey said: "Brought Rover to have a look at you, Rockie. He was getting on my tits." Having made sure that door and half-door were shut, he slipped the leash.

The dog knew the form, he'd been this way before. Already quietened by Rockie's looming presence, he padded across to whine up at him plaintively. The horse blew down his nose. Mr. Watson-Harvey slipped out of the door, bolting it and the separate upper half behind him.

What he did not know, and could not see in the dark, was that the bolt securing the latter did not home properly in the pit dug into the jamb to receive it, without the door's being lifted a little. Wood is a material subject over the years to saggage and shrinkage. Fiona and her mother knew what to do; but horses were not Mr. Watson-Harvey's thing, and he seldom went near the stable. So he simply shot the bolt and walked away, leaving that upper half only semi-secure, held shut more by the return spring than by the bolt.

It is not in the nature of dogs to keep a stiff upper lip. In distress, when they have poured out the heart to whoever is available, man or horse, or to nobody and the moon if that is all the company, they begin to scratch and paw and leap at whatever impediment they believe stands between them and heart's desire. Almost before Mr. Watson-Harvey had reported back to his wife and settled again to his bread-winning, Rover had told his troubles to the horse, who was a good listener; and scratched and pawed and leaped at the door; and found, when the jarring totally cleared the bolt, that the top half opened. It closed again, on the spring, but it definitely opened. Quick as a flash he was up and through it, gone without so much as farewell. The horse sighed, stamped, and relieved himself mournfully where he stood.

The Doberman is a good hunting dog. This one bounded over the garden gate and straight as an arrow along the path Fiona had taken. Black nose down, whining eagerly he raced down the road, along the path bordering the field that held the sheep, and into the yard-cum-patio; and here, where Fiona got into the car with the twins, he lost her scent. She went to the French windows; she came out again among other scents that he knew because he had been here often enough and the boys called at his home, and had done ever since he was a pup.

It was obvious what had happened. He rode often in cars, he knew what they were used for. Here where the human scents vanished was the nose-tingling stink of a car.

They had taken her away. Again. Oh, this was by no means the first time. If it was not they who took her away, himself abandoned in the kitchen and she all dressed up, how was it always they who brought her back, after his time of misery?

Perhaps—just perhaps she was still inside. Knowing in his heart that she was not, he nevertheless scratched and whined at the windows, even called to her at the door, one long howl like a lost and starving wolf. Upstairs in her bed Mrs. Wellington slept on in her mix of Valium and vodka, not hearing a thing.

He cast around for a time; and then, because he needed her scent and at the same time to be on the move, he back-tracked a little. To the path; from where he saw the sheep.

He knew these bloody sheep, he knew who they belonged to.

He'd stood by eyeing the daft things many times while Fiona talked with one or both of the boys working among them; restrained by her sharp command from seeing what happened if you leaped upon them roaring. Many and many a time he had side-squinted them, feeling his teeth itch and his mouth water.

She wouldn't like it. She wouldn't like it. He paced up and down by the field gate, blood and guilt locked in sudden, uprushing combat. She wouldn't like it, if she were here she would be saying sit; and again, if he could not force himself at once to obey: SIT!!

But: she was not here. And why? Because the bastards who owned these daft bastards had taken her away, that's why.

Blood won, helped perhaps by his need for natural activity to divert his hurting mind. In times of stress, sophisticated life-forms seek ease and self-stabilizing instinctively in what they do best, obedient to their nature. Riven still with guilt he slipped through the gatebars, coming onto the nearest sheep like a black silent ghost, snapping with a sudden growl at the wooly back leg.

The sheep and all the sheep began to run, frightening the night with their panicking voices. He tasted the wool, the flesh, the blood, he felt the surge of his power; and the lust took over. He released the leg, made two fast strides and went for the throat.

Three minutes later he slipped again through the gate, leaving behind him three sheep dead and two dying amid the cacophony of terror. He'd have killed the lot; but guilt came back, even in the very heat of his snarling lust. She wouldn't like it—he shouldn't be doing it. Rip them—gash them—kill them, howled his blood. She wouldn't like it, said his heart. He truly worshipped that girl. She frowned in his soul, saying sit. Even a dog, once civilised, cannot obey his inner nature fully, held in guilty check by his inhibiting religion.

Nobody saw him go. Probably nobody heard the frenzied bleating. There was a soccer international on television, and village women seldom go out at night, even the in-comer surburban ones. If anybody did hear they took no notice, so they were not country-born; and Mrs. Wellington would have slept with the bed going up in flames and the masonry crashing about her, the state she was in.

So he came back along the path, along the road and in again through that swinging half-door unseen except by the horse, at whom he looked for a long time, elated with killing and torn with guilt, wondering how it would feel to sink his teeth into that smoother, bigger, silkier throat.

They stopped on the way to town in a layby, where another car waited. Simon handed over the larger package, not needing even to get out because a man strolled across and took it through the window. Nobody had to hurry, there was no other traffic about. On the Hutton Fellows road there seldom is, after dark. By the time the man got back to his car they were on their way again, headed for town and the disco called the Laughing Jackass. The other car, as soon as the man rejoined his mate in it, drove off in the opposite direction until it turned right at the fork leading to the big city and beyond, all the way up until the heather, the kilt and the sporran give way to a sullen sea. No wonder the bent get rich. How can your police cover all the lonely places, Lands End to John o' Groats.

But not every operation is carried out in a lonely place. Take drug distribution, bottom end. A line of young junkies queuing at a car in a layby might well attract comment. So a chain of recognised passing places is set up, and some are remarkably public.

Discos, roadhouses on Saturday nights, some pubs and many clubs are not lonely. They are favoured, some of them, without the management being necessarily aware of it, by people who pass the stuff not to the poor little bastard hooked, probably ragged and with nothing left but twitches and an agonised need to fix, anywhere no matter how, or the gaunt little girl with mad eyes who learned to earn the price by knicker-dropping until nobody wanted even that from her anymore; but to the people who deal with these and all the in-betweens down from just starting and still looking healthy. Nice, normal looking-people, many very young. The latter favour discos, the older and more sophisticated fit better into the roadhouses and pubs.

The Laughing Jackass rarely gives the police much trouble. It stands in the town centre in a wide street called George Square, plenty of parking space handy after the shops and offices close for the jalopies and motorbikes that stand about all evening while the owners, borrowers from Dad, and those who came on pillions or in passenger seats leap about amid dim lighting to the ear-shattering records favoured by them and a disc jockey called Boo Boo Texas Frank. Strange American accent. Comes from Birmingham. Simon eased the car into an empty space close by the entrance. Three nice-looking young people walked into the cacophony, where Detective Sergeant Henry Panton was already ensconced.

6

When Sergeant Panton left the station earlier he had in mind a quiet evening at home with the television set, one ear cocked to the telephone in case it should ring to summon him back to work. If it didn't: a little of his mother's justly famous cold pork-beagle for supper and early to bed, clothes folded handy for ease of leaping into and a packet of sandwiches in his executive case. A man may carry an executive case without actually being an executive. They are on open sale in all good stores.

After the big match, at the very start of a movie in a series called *Another Chance to See* in tacit admission that every sighted male or female in the country must have seen it already, at least twice, as his mother turned the heel of a sock (and what a knitter she was) the phone did ring. "I'll take it, love," he said, and left Gary Cooper getting married to Grace Kelly.

A whispering voice spoke out of the phone. "Hallo. Who's that?"

"All right, Willie," he said. "It's me."

"Ah—Mr. Panton," the whisper said. Every grass whispers, even in a public phone booth. It's a statement of their unease. They lead a terrible life. "That caper. You know. I can tell you something interesting."

"Uh-huh. When?"

"Tonight."

It must be emphasised: until he is actually assigned to a

murder case or other big felony, a C.I.D. man does not drop all his other work. He would be in trouble if he did, without specific orders to do so. And this little man had been a long time whispering. Now that he had, he could not be handed over. A grass will normally cooperate only with one officer who has won, if not his trust, at least his panicky respect. "Where, and what time?"

"Laughing Jackass. About half eight." The little man was gone.

Sergeant Panton broke the connection with a finger and rang the station, so that they would know he was off to the Laughing Jackass. On a job. So if you need me, he said, don't just ring and ask for a message to be passed on. Which was fair enough, you cannot have anonymity for self and grass blown by some prat braying over the disco intercom or Boo Boo Texas Frank bellowing through his mike. If they need you, let them send a man in plain clothes to wink from a nearby table. And let him arrive in a plain van.

He was back in the living room almost before Cooper knew there were baddies on the train, coming to get him; saying to his mother and his father too: "Have to go out. Something's come up."

"I don't see why you stay with it," his father said. "If you'd gone in with your Uncle Fred you'd have been finished at half-past five."

"What a pity, dear," said his mother over the clicking of Number Nine needles. "Shall I cut you a piece of cake?"

"No thanks, Mum, I've got the sandwiches. Leave a bit of pork-beagle out, if you go to bed before I'm back." He dropped a kiss on her forehead. He was fond of his Mum.

"Didn't hear you say please," his father said.

"What for?"

"Pork-beagle. When you want something left out in this house, you say please."

"Ah. Please." He was fond of his Dad, too.

Almost exactly at half-past eight he entered the Laughing Jackass, bought himself a coke and sat down at one of the tables surrounding a central dancing space, already well peopled. Policemen are, of course, much younger than they used to be, and in the leisure jacket donned before leaving home he fitted quite nicely into the ambience. He sat and sipped his coke until, only a few minutes later, his little man appeared.

A presentable youth, as youths go. Quite good looking, really. Not every grass slinks about with furtive eyes and hair growing out of the nostrils. Very few do, in fact. Villains worth shopping are usually snappy dressers, and your grass is, or has been, one of the cognoscenti, playing the double game now for his own benefit. This one hailed Sergeant Panton brightly, and loudly to get on top of the music. Whispering here would be waste of lip-muscle. And noticeable.

"Hi, man—how's your sex life?"

"Getting my share," said Sergeant Panton, who really wasn't, and hadn't since Suzy threw him aside because (a) how could they have any social life, the crazy hours he worked; (b) half his mind was on his job all the time, except when they were actually doing it; and (c) she'd had enough of him anyway, and there was this brown-eyed average adjuster who made a lot of money adjusting averages.

"Stick around, man," the grass cried. His name was Baggin. Clifford Baggin, but Willie in dealings with the sergeant. He chose it, for the sake of privacy.

He crossed to the soft drinks bar—the Laughing Jackass has no liquor license—to gather a Coke, or a Pepsi, or something else with beaded bubbles winking at the brim, and while he was there the twins arrived with Fiona, who, when she had handed in her cashmere shawl, showed herself briefly at the top of the steps that lead down from tabled level to dance floor before vanishing into the ladies' lavatory. The twins moved in the dim light to a table on the far side of the hall from where the sergeant sat with his back to the entrance.

Clifford Baggin returned, crying more merrily yet for the benefit of those who might be within earshot—they were groping and

52

snogging and attending to their own egos, not caring a damn: "O.K., man—let's hear it, if it's so good." He sat down.

Five minutes later, the sergeant knew all about a forthcoming warehouse job. He knew the names of all the involved, he knew the time and place of their meeting and what transport they would be using, even from which overnight park they intended to annex the necessary truck, returning it after the job by arrangement with the driver who would stay in his lettie, watching telly.

What he did not know was that four or five young ladies went one by one into the lavatory and came out with packets in their jeans, those who wore them, or stuffed in their bras, those who wore them, or otherwise concealed about their persons. The knickers is a favoured place, among those who wear them. Last out was Fiona, her handbag now containing a great deal of money.

Four or five young ladies going to the loo are not in themselves matter for concentrated conjecture, even though each follows pretty closely upon the heels of another. The sergeant, attention fixed on the lad Baggins, did not notice them. Nor did he see—and if he had, in that dim and flickering light would not have recognised—Fiona, when she emerged and made her way to the table where the twins were sitting, pausing en route to exchange badinage with a group of youngsters. He sat entirely concentrated upon the grassing; which was difficult enough to hear because of the musical din.

Things like this cannot be shouted, exactly; but parodoxically, loud noise is good cover. In quiet places, people can overhear. Which is why many grasses refuse meetings in places where the birds sing, choosing always to divulge in public places where the fun is fast and furious.

So Sergeant Panton was not giving the trio met earlier in the day a single thought when he saw Fiona, suddenly undulating on the floor. She had delivered her handbag back to the twins' table, where Simon took it over while Timothy led her out to dance. The music was braying, their customers were gone, eager to further adulterate those already adulterated packets and set about recouping the investment. The rest of the night was their own, not a sniff of junk left in the Laughing Jackass. Maybe a bit of grass here and there, but they were clean again.

He did not at first recognise her, dressed as she was and in that flickering coloured light. Firmly heterosexual, he was, so the lad she danced with failed altogether to register upon an eye that wandered idly, as the eye of a good man should in a disco, among writhing peach-buttocks and jouncing breasts while he memorised—he could hardly take notes. Not here—all the details he must pass on to the station. The buttocks under the tight black velvet, the breasts above rotated and bounced as vigourously as any, and more elegantly than most. When his eyes got as far as the face, he thought: I know her; and then: it's that what's her name— Watson-Hargraves. Fiona.

She noticed him almost at the same time and he saw her visibly start, check for a moment in her cavorting. Even in the dimness flicking through green, to red, to blue and back to green he saw her mouth half open. Then she smiled, tentatively. He smiled back, raising a hand in salute.

Immediately, his little man stiffened. "Do you know her?" he demanded; meaning: does she know you, and what you are?

The sergeant lied. To a grass, any unexpected happening poses a threat. It takes a long time and a lot of work to inculcate trust in one. To find himself at a table under eyes that know his companion for a detective can send one scuttling down his hole, never to come out again. Not even for money. "No," the policeman said. "I was looking at her, and she gave me the come-on."

Well, it happens all the time. That's what discoteques are for. Soothed somewhat, the lad said: "Fancy it?" he very nearly leered.

Sergeant Panton did. Nor was he alone in this, and that was the root of her psychological problems, as it is with most too-beautiful young girls. So he made no bones about it. "You kidding? Cor!" His eyes were still upon Fiona, who was speaking to her partner as she danced.

54

"No sweat," said Clifford Baggin. "They reckon she's a right raver. Anything with a prick."

"Who says?" And was she? She didn't look like it this morning, she looked as if butter wouldn't melt between her legs. But—mm—she was chucking it about tonight. The lad with her was glancing over his shoulder. At him, Sergeant Panton.

"Well—you know. Everybody. Lives out at Hutton Fellows, I got a mate there. Reckons she'll drop 'em anywhere. Geezer she's with, he's got a twin brother. They reckon they both have her, one at a time or the old meat sandwich. Them and anybody else who comes handy. She's got a bloody great dog."

The sergeant steered away from the subject. A young policeman working among the young does not establish and maintain contact by shying away from modern sexual attitudes, but it can go too far. To join in sniggering is to lose respect; and to lose respect is to lose grip. Oddly old-fashioned in their attitude to the police, the little people are.

It could all be true—sneaky little men know most of what is going on around them. That was certainly one or other of the Wellington twins with her. And why not, they lived close and knew each other. None of his business, anyway. His business was to keep his mind on his business. He had already slipped his little friend the crinkling envelope. Now he said:

"Well—we'd better break this up. Much obliged to you, Cliff. Who's leaving first, you or me?"

"I'll stick around for a bit," the grass said. He'd probably get a bit, too, if that's what he meant. Not bad looking, money in his pocket and all.

The sergeant stood up. "See you, then. You know where to get me, any time you've got a little something." And he left, well satisfied with his evening's work.

Pity, really. Normal official approval might be doled out for his handling of the warehouse caper; but think of the kudos that must have accrued had he come back from this jaunt with not one little cracker, but two. And one of them a drugs lurk. On such little strokes are great careers founded.

Almost before he was through the exit, Fiona left the floor and made for the table where Simon sat. Behind her came Timothy, in less of a hurry. She said: "We've got to get out. We've got to go home. I said we shouldn't have come."

"Hold it, hold it," the young man said. He glanced at his brother. Timothy grinned almost ruefully, and shrugged his shoulders. "Calm down—calm down."

"Never mind calm down," she said. "That sergeant was here."

"What sergeant?"

Timothy spoke. "The one who was with the Monkeyman."

"He's watching us," Fiona said. "I told you they would, didn't I? We've got to go."

Now the twins were not complete idiots; but all their lives, as sons of a weak widow, they had done whatever they wanted, in complete rapport. This kind of alliance, when it turns evil, turns very evil indeed, as witness the Kray brothers; and the strength of its evil, the root of its overwheening self-confidence, is in the confirmation each gives the other that no retribution can come to them since they were born to be more handsome, more intelligent and highly favoured than their fellow-man, given carte blanche by whatever gods may be to pursue their own ends, and nobody to say them nay. In truth, these two gained mutual pleasure from riding on regardless over anyone who tried.

Nobody, in fact, had ever seriously tried. In public they were as well behaved as young men should be—it amused them to be so, they enjoyed pulling wool over eyes. People said they were spoiled, of course, but nice enough lads in spite of it, surprisingly so considering their mother, but nobody knew the things they got up to. There was a certain amount of whispering about their sex life; but this among the young, who keep such things from their elders, at least in Hutton Fellows, where the telly-fed young are locked in constant battle with their peers over what is right and proper. Whisper said they had it away with Fiona, double-banked

56

or treble. And this was all right with the young, who if they were not themselves having it away and keeping quiet about it were trying very hard to. Two of the ravenous young males had tapped Fiona out for themselves. Some said they made it, some said it was all brag; but now she was known as anybody's crump.

In every alliance there is a leader; and in spite of the facade that presented them as virtually indentical in mental force as in appearance, in this case it was Simon. He said now: "Come down, come down, you'll get your knickers all wet. Sit down and have a Coke."

"I don't want a Coke, I don't want to sit down." As spoiled as they were, but without their self-confidence. And so, perilously excitable.

The look came into Simon's eye. No doubt it came into Timothy's, behind her. "Sit down!"

She knew the look, had seen it often, long before the day when they led her into their bedroom and showed her what they could do for her and she for them, their mother drunk downstairs. To the look, straight and steely and doubly impressive in duplicate, was owed much of their dominion over her. That, and her need to be dominated, unfulfilled at home. And the sexual hunger that stays always in a girl toward her first partner, if he (or they) be skilled, and which these two kept feverish by teasing and touching and only slaking as and when it suited them. If she did not love these lads—and what spoiled child can love?—she was certainly subservient to them, and had been for years. She sat down. So did Timothy.

"Now then," said Simon, "stop getting hysterical. All the stuff's gone—we're clean."

"What about—in my handbag?"

"Nobody can touch your handbag. They can't touch *anything*. Have a Coke. We're staying. We carry on as usual. Come on—if you're going to twitch, do it on the dance floor."

No need for Timothy to say a single word, his thinking was Simon's thinking. No problem—the copper just happened to be here. Lots of people came here, it was a great pickup point. He was probably after grumble. Even if he wasn't: stay, and act exactly as usual. He couldn't have anything on them.

They kept her dancing, and left in time to be home by midnight. They delivered her, smiling nicely upon her mother, who answered the door. Neither of her parents ever went to bed before she was safely back in the bosom. Her father looked up from the programme he seemed to be watching, his books still beside him, worked at until an hour ago. "Hallo, Chick-chick," he said. "Had a good time?"

"Fine, Daddy," Fiona said. "Lovely."

"*I* think you look a little pale," said Mrs. Watson-Harvey. "I wouldn't be surprised if you are overdoing it. Perhaps we should ask Dr. Pinky for a tonic."

"Oh, for heaven's sake, Mother."

"Your mummy could be right." Mr. Watson-Harvey began to gather up his work. Well used to sublimating his own feelings in this house, it would have taken subtle observation to detect that he was a very worried man. "You do look a little washed out. A bottle of something couldn't do any harm." So did he, but nobody much bothers about washed-out fathers.

"A teeny tiny supper, darling," said Mrs. Watson-Harvey, "and off you go to Bedfordshire. Better just go and fetch Rover in, Daddy."

The twins were turning in at their gate by now. They left the car in the yard, entered the house, ate a little something and went to bed, not bothering to look in upon their mother, who owed her condition largely to them. So long as she was kept tottering there was nobody to query their activities, in or out of the house. Over the years they had smilingly encouraged her in a natural predilection for the bottle, topping up her glass whenever it was empty ("Such good boys," she said. "How you do look after your mother") and lacing it of late, since the need for secrecy increased, with tablets and dribbles of white powder out of stock. They slept quite soundly, with no idea that four of their sheep were dead and a fifth well on the way.

7

The next morning, at about the time when the boys found out about the sheep, Detective Inspector Rosher sat in the Chief's oak-panelled office, trying not to make noises as he sipped coffee from a ridiculous dwarf cup, one hairy end finger stuck out, or to drop crumbs when he bit into a Huntley and Palmer.

He was not the only officer present. Every Chief Constable holds a morning conference with his top investigators when a major case is under way, though not all of them serve coffee and biscuits. This was the Chief's own idea. Nobody liked it very much. Many sighed back to the days when the old bastard as was would have seen the tongue swell up purple before he offered a minion a thimble of water. You knew where you were in those days, they said.

Detective Superintendent Bishop was here, and Chief Superintendent Rollie Rawlins, whose men were still working. There is a lot of footslogging done, in a murder case. Various specialists were here, some of them deplorably scruffy. Detective Inspector Cruse was here; and the Chief, who handled coffee and biscuits with casual skill, was saying: "It seems to be one of those cases where there is very little to go on. We've searched the entire area without uncovering the weapon. Not that we necessarily won't, but we haven't up to now. And there are too many footprints on that path for any to be useful." The search was still going on, of course, in and around the woods. "Nobody that we know of seems to have any motive, and the consensus of opinion leans toward impulse killing. Which *might* suggest, if it suggests anything at all, that this mentally unbalanced friend might be able to help us. This what's-his-name—Tom Bola."

"Nolan, sir," said Detective Inspector Cruse. "Tom Nolan."

"Nolan, yes. And we have been unable to trace him, as yet. Gone from his normal haunts, and you, Mr. Cruse, believe he is sleeping rough."

"He's known to do so."

All the Chief was doing, of course, was marking time. They were all marking time. Until something came back from somewhere, there was nothing they could do but ensure that the teams in the field were functioning efficiently and go over again and again all the known facts, seeking some little thing everybody could be overlooking.

Superintendent Bishop spoke up. "We've got a general call out for him, sir. Problem is, no pictures." A picture wired to every force in the country is a great help, in a search like this. Trouble with vagrants: they get about. They can hitch-hike from one end of the land to the other, they can stop off at any point between. So long as they do not draw police attention and avoid the known haunts where layabouts gather, it can be one helluva job to clap hands upon them.

"What are your thoughts, Mr. Rosher?" the Chief asked. He liked to engage the full company.

Rosher had no thoughts at the moment bearing upon the case. He knew when it was profitable to think about work and when it was not. All his attention was given to steering that daft little cup and hoping the handle would not fall off between his banana fingers. Many working policemen detest fragile china, which has a tendency to disintegrate embarrassingly. They prefer the security of a good, solid-sided mug. But no policeman admits, to top brass or anybody else, that his mind is not devoted to his work. So he said: "I don't see that we can move very far in the matter at present, sir. Everything's being done that can be done, it's just a matter of keeping at it until the break comes."

60

Statement of the very obvious; but then, the situation itself was obvious. He made the speech only because the Chief, of his courtesy, called upon him.

"True," the top dog said. "Very true. Well—you will keep me closely informed, Mr. Bishop, of course. More coffee, anyone? Mr. Rosher?"

"No thank you, sir," said Rosher, hastily. He returned his little cup to the tray, carefully and with great relief. The meeting was over. Now, perhaps, they could get some bloody work done.

Sheep, unlike cows and nanny goats, do not have to be milked. Nobody had to get up in the pearly dawn to bring them ease. They stand about in fields and chew, that's all. Agreed, they have to be dipped from time to time and sheared down to the underwear and guarded against various ticks and footrot; but nobody shears or dips in October, and the other tasks can be approached leisurely, at any time of the day. Wherefore, the twins were at breakfast when old Ossie Horrick tapped on the French window.

Old Ossie was a casual farm labourer. Had been all his life. Born here, of a father who earned six shillings and sixpence for dawn to dark work in fields belonging then to the Lord of the Manor, and brought up twelve children on it. Old Ossie was the twelfth. His Dad would never have known him now, all gnarled and bent and warty, standing at the tarted-up window and saying: "Do 'ee know some o' your ole sheep is dead?"

"What?" said Timothy, who had come to the window. "How do you mean, dead?"

"Dead, ayn' they?" said Old Ossie, squinting upward and showing his tooth. Not in a smile, it just happened when he squinted upward. "In yore ole field. Big an ole dog got at 'em, I rackon. That ayn' no good, is ut?"

It is not good, when a dog gets among sheep. It is very, very bad. Bad for the sheep, bad for the farmer. And it is by no means uncommon. The dog is fundamentally a vicious killer and there are five million of them in England, many owned by the besotted who indignantly refused to believe it of them. Once, a country dog was tied up and sternly disciplined, kept as a working tool by a man who knew him well. But most cottage-dwellers now are transplanted suburbanites. They call their doggies Fido and would *never* tie then up. Would we, Boysie? Who's a lovely Boysie, den? Who loves his Mummy? Walkies!

Simon was here now, leaving the bacon to congeal on the table. The mother wouldn't eat it up, she hadn't left her bed yet. Together, the twins stepped out and made for the field, Old Ossie creaming along in their wake on legs bandy to a degree that put Inspector Rosher's to very shame. Such legs on old farm labourers are not a gift direct from God. They have to be worked for over eighty years, building on a foundation of malnutrition.

The sheep were undoubtedly dead, stiff by now and bloodily mutilated. Old Ossie, catching up, said: "I wooden've seed 'em, hadn't bin fer the crows." Crows like carcasses, they peck out he eyes. Some were doing it now.

"Bastard!" said Simon. "Bloody bastard!"

He spoke for all. For Old Ossie, because every countryman knows it for a bastard, when a dog takes to ripping up sheep; for his brother and himself because: well—the sheep were theirs. They had no feeling for them, they were touched by no pity; but the sheep were *theirs*; and what was theirs no man or dog or act of God or nature must destroy or otherwise interfere with. They stood with the look in their eyes, faces suddenly fierce and implacable, looking at their dead sheep. Sheep kept partly as cover, presenting a reason why they stayed on the farm to work, and partly because they had an interest in breeding for improvement, and prizes.

Old Ossie broke the silence. "Mr. Jackson, 'ee 'ad some done. August, that were." Mr. Jackson ran sheep in the hills, five miles away.

"Bastard," Simon said again. The living sheep were busy cropping; staying away from their dead brethren but caring not a damn about them, really.

"You'll have to tell the police," gummed Ossie. "You'll have to tell young Ted Phillis." The local copper. Didn't live in the village, which has no resident constable. Drove through in his little van from time to time, just to keep an eye on things. And young? Fifty, if a day.

Simon brought out a roll of notes, peeled off a fiver and gave it to the old man. "Thanks for letting us know, Ossie," he said. "Buy yourself a drink."

"Oo, ta," said Old Ossie. To an aged man, until he comes to spend it, a fiver is a fortune. When he was young you could buy a cow and a smallholding with a fiver, and enjoy the warmest women for miles around, and still have enough left for a right old booze-up on the Saturday night. "Want me to tell young Ted?"

"We'll see to it. Nothing you can do—I should get back to work."

"Ar. I'll drink your health, when I had me dinner." The old man toddled away as swiftly as he could twinkle, before somebody realised the fiver was not a pound note and snatched it back.

Timothy said, when they were alone: "Bugger it. What do you think we ought to do?"

"Bury 'em," said his brother, briefly.

"We ought to report it to the police, really."

"Sod the police. They're our sheep, we don't want the bloody police nosing around. Get 'em under."

"That silly old sod'll have it all over the village in half an hour. We should have told him to keep his mouth shut."

"Wouldn't have done any good, he'd just have told everybody not to say anything because we told him to keep it dark. It'll be all over the village anyway." It is true, of course. You can't keep a farming calamity quiet in a village.

"Bloody nuisance," said Timothy. "I'm not sure we shouldn't let old Ted Phillis know. He's harmless, and he wouldn't have to come near the house. Not that we've got anything to worry about if he did."

"We'll sort it out when we've buried 'em."

"Shouldn't we leave 'em where they are, until he's seen 'em?"

"If he wants to see them he can dig 'em up. They're our

bloody sheep, we can do what we like with 'em. Let's get the spades."

They walked back to the barn used as storage place for the various tools a sheep farmer needs and as garage for the small truck they could drive about with impunity. No man making a living from sheep, or any other kind of farming, can function without a truck.

Arrogance, of course. Nobody was going to tell them what to do with their own. Certainly they were not going to leave dead sheep gathering flies and crows in their field until a hobbledehoy village copper chose to appear. Arrogance; and chiming in with it, simple caution. They had too many secrets to relish repeated contact with the police. They were not worried, in any way. But neither were they idiots.

Perhaps because anger at the outraging of their predatory instincts combined with this arrogance to focus them on the happening itself, they gave never a thought to what dog did it. Dogs savage sheep, there are always dogs about. Farmers shoot them, they mount a watch or get up a hunt if it happens as more than an isolated incident.

Had they thought about dogs, they would have dismissed Rover. Rover was never allowed out alone; always, he came with Fiona, controlled not only by her firmness but by his own doting. Her lightest word was his command. Most civilised dog in the area, so long as no one seemed to threaten the beloved.

Detective Inspector Rosher was considering lunch when the visitors arrived. He had been thinking throughout the morning about the death of Edward Poddy, and one or two other matters because there was not sufficient fibre in that one for the mind to grind the teeth against. Now he was thinking of lunch, when his intercom buzzed and the pleasant voice of Sergeant Barney Dancey, an altogether pleasant policeman, spoke when he flipped the switch from the little glassed-in office labelled Reception.

"Alf? There's Mr. and Mrs. Poddy, asking to see you. Personally."

"Ah. What do they want?" Only one man called Rosher by his forename, and that was Barney. Some called him Old Blubbergut, or That Thick Old Bastard, or to his face Inspector. Even Mr. Rosher. Nobody but Barney called him Alf. And he called nobody by their fore or nick name. Except Barney. He called Barney Barney.

"To see you. Personally."

"All right, Barney." Here he was, doing it. "Keep 'em there, I'll be down. Is Bishop back?"

"Nope."

"Right." And he flipped the switch.

Superintendent Bishop, restless because the onus was on him as chief investigating officer to keep the case moving, had gone back to the scene of the crime to see that the squad still sniffing there peered at every stick, every stone, every blade of grass and inch of leaf-mouldy earth. They had done it by now many times, and had established only that no fight took place on the path. They might do it many more times, trying to find the elusive something. It is not so easy as you think. The presence of high brass does not help; but high brass thinks it does, and when no other aspect of the matter keeps it elsewhere you will find it pacing the area, hands behind the back and brooding.

So Archie Bishop was away to the woods; and this left Rosher exactly where he liked to be: all on his own and unsupervised when something stirred, asking for him personally. It could be the initial tweak, the little nibble they had all been casting about for.

When he had licked his fingers and smoothed down the hair at the sides of his durable skull he left his office and claked along the corridor to the reception area. There stood the Poddys, looking smaller than they did at home; pale and sadly vulnerable, dressed in decent black as befits mourning parents who worship a black-clad God. Mr. Poddy carried a neat package under his arm, about the size and shape of a shoe-box. The inspector said, jovially: "Ah, Mrs. Poddy. How are you? Good morning, Mr. Poddy."

"Good morning, Mr. Rosher," they both said.

"You wanted to see me?"

"Yes. Yes," they said; and Mrs. Poddy added, almost timourously: "It's—about a—rather private matter."

"We'll go to my office, shall we? Anybody wants me, Barney, I'm tied up with Mr. and Mrs. Poddy."

A younger, cheekier policeman might have said "Oh—kinky," but Barney long ago passed being young and cheeky and came at last to where he was now: sadder, perhaps, and probably wiser if only in knowledge of human depravity; and yet with baby-blue eyes retaining an innocent faith. God knows how he'd managed it, over thirty years in a police force. He said: "Right ho, Inspector." Eschewing the Alf, to favour the public image. And he bent his head, applying his ballpoint to a fresh page of his big, black Incidents Book.

Mr. Rosher led the way, clacking back over the compo flooring. If the visitors clacked less it was because they lacked his boxy-toed footwear. When they reached his office he said, spraying them liberally with that charm which gave him the aspect of an enthusiastic gorilla: "Sit down, won't you? Oh—you can't. We need another chair. Hang on a minute."

He fetched a chair from the corridor. There were always a few standing about out there. When he brought it in, Mr. Poddy was already unwrapping his package. "Sit down, sit down," the inspector said. Mrs. Poddy was seated already, on the one wooden chair in front of his desk. He positioned the one brought in beside it and sat himself in his own swivel chair, facing them benignly across the desk. "Now—what can one do for you?"

Mr. Poddy sat. It was indeed a shoebox he carried, revealed as the brown paper came away. "It's about—this," he said. "We came across it when we were clearing Teddy's room out. Well, my wife—Mrs. Poddy—did." He half rose, to proffer the box.

Inspector Rosher took it. He removed the lid. It was filled with money. Paper money, a thick layer of old notes above several packets of new ones. The loose layer was a mixture of denominations, one pound and five pound. The packets were all fives. "Ah," he said. Joviality dropped from him. A sterner gorilla looked up at

66

them over the old oak desk. "Where did you find this, madam?" he asked.

Mrs. Poddy was sitting very stiffly upright; the mother-eagle look back on her face, initial timidity engendered by unfamiliar, bleakly official surroundings quite gone. "On top of his wardrobe," she snapped. Her eyes challenged him.

"There are cases up there," said Mr. Poddy. Fathers are less fierce than mothers. It was not their body torn in giving birth. They tend to adopt a conciliatory manner, faced with a stern gorilla. Respectable ones do. "One inside the other. It was in the smallest."

"Uh-huh. How much is here?"

"We haven't counted it, we thought we shouldn't—touch it too much. We thought we'd better—come and see you."

"Quite right, sir. Quite right. Very commendable. Do you have any idea how your son came by so much money?"

"No. He never had any. To speak of."

"It appears, sir, that he did."

"Yes. But I—we—can't think how." He added, in a burst of painful candour: "We used to, as a matter of fact, we used to leave money about for him. He used to . . . steal it. . . ."

"It was his illness," Mrs. Poddy snapped. "His illness."

"God visited him with suffering," said Mr. Poddy. "He preferred to steal it. We never told him we left it for him to . . . to take—"

"How much?" the inspector said.

"Beg pardon?"

"How much did you leave about? Large sums?"

"Oh no. No. A few pounds here and there. Five. Sometimes ten. When he seemed to be in need of it."

"He was a good boy," said Mrs. Poddy. "He simply couldn't— It was his illness." Tears stood suddenly in the hurt and hostile eyes.

Oh, so much stress and misery passes through police stations. They had not been allowed even to bury their dead.

"You are unable to offer any explanation at all?"

"No. It was a complete shock," said Mr. Poddy. "It came as a shock. It was obviously something you should know about."

It was indeed. A helluva lot of money there. Rosher looked at it; not touching, because the fingerprint and forensic boys might want a go at it. Where would a lad get all that poppy? There are many interesting methods for accumulating cases full of folding, none of them honest. And few of them open to those who blow the top at intervals.

"Had he got rich friends?" Because in this wicked world you never know—somebody might have entrusted it to him. To evade taxes. Not likely; but then, look at the capers around Buckingham Palace. Not much likely about that, everybody turning out to be spies and queer with it. Little men squatting on the Queen's bed supping plonk.

"Not that we know of." Mr. Poddy was obviously chief spokesman; but Mrs. Poddy was the fiercer.

"Mm. Is there anything else? Passbooks, bank statements?"

"He didn't have a bank account," Mr. Poddy said. He added: "So far as we know."

"Uh-huh. I take it you have looked through all his possessions?"

"No. Mother—Mrs. Poddy—had only just started straightening up. She found this and brought it down. We came in straightaway."

"I take it you would have no objection if I took a run out to look at his stuff?" Do the place over, is the technical term; but you don't use it in communion with the general public.

Mrs. Poddy opened her mouth, as if to object; shut it again into a straight line. Her husband hesitated a moment before he said: "No. No. We want to do—everything we can."

"Thank you," said Rosher. "You understand that we will have to take charge of this for now, don't you? You will be given a receipt, of course."

"Yes. Of course."

Let them go now, the inspector thought. Get out there. You

can sort it out with them better on the spot if anything else turns up. He got to his feet, holding the box. "If you will step this way," he said, "we'll get it counted and issue a receipt."

"Is that all?" said Mr. Poddy.

"For now, sir, yes. Unless the Chief Constable would like a word with you. This way, if you please."

There are three interview rooms lining that passage back to the reception area. Two are little bastards, all sick-mustard paint and containing only a stark desk and a couple of wooden chairs standing on a stone floor, one tiny barred window high up. The other is carpeted, with a comfortable settee, two nice armchairs and pictures on the bright walls. Another of the new Chief Constable's innovations, springing from humane consideration for the bereaved, the robbery victims, the mugged, the mentally shocked or distressed who pass through police hands day by day. They are not criminals, he said. I wouldn't want my mother stuck in one of these little cells. And bash another window in the wall.

Into this oasis in a desert of soggy-spinach green and sick-mustard Rosher ushered the Poddys. "Make yourselves comfortable," he suggested, knowing it was the one place in the station where they could. "I'll be back in a minute." He shut them in and clacked on to the reception desk, where he said to Sergeant Dancey: "Got somebody to hand over to, Barney? Want you to come with me, count this lot." He indicated the box.

"What's in it?" Barney asked.

"Bloody fortune."

"Bung ho. Maybe some of it'll stick."

"I'll just use your intercom, have a word with the Old Man."

Nobody had to tell Sergeant Barney to bring cotton gloves, one pair for him and one for Rosher. The Chief Constable came down while they were counting, the notes making a lovely rustling in the quiet room. He spoke with charm to the Poddys, who had elected to sit side-by-side on the settee. This was his forte, this genuine sympathy with hurt people. A prime example: his re-elevation of Rosher to some sort of dignity (and full pension rights) from the sergeant's desk to which he had been fastened by the short and curlies.

If he did not now keep the Poddys happy, he certainly did nothing to increase their unhappiness while the notes were counted; and this took a fair time. At last Inspector Rosher totted up his scribbled figures and pushed the pad over to Barney for checking. "Nine thousand, seven hundred and eighty-five," he said.

And now there was the receipt to be made out, signed and countersigned and handed over. There was Rosher, the money back in the box, tucking it under his arm, bidding farewell to the Poddys and telling them, before he bandied away to Forensic, that he would be along shortly. And the Chief Constable seeing the Poddys off in person, assuring them on the front step that everything was being done that could be done and that it was just a matter of time. He came back in with a tract.

In the Forensic Department, Inspector Benny (Stinkfinger) Clarke said to Inspector Rosher: "Christ Almighty—that lot'll take days to get through. We'll have to treat the lot with Nilhildrin."

Well, treating with Nilhildrin can be a laborious process, the paper needing to be dipped and developed like a photograph. But nothing says you must dip each sheet or banknote singly, you can hang them on racks and do them in batches. It wouldn't take days. Just another copper with his funny little ways. "Better get on with it, then, hadn't you?" said Rosher. "I want a receipt for that lot. And it's all counted."

He got his receipt and went back to his office. Only when he got there did it come to him that he had sent no word to Superintendent Bishop, nosing about in the woods. Good job it wasn't Percy, there'd have been arse-kicking done. He made radio contact, right away.

70

8

When Detective Chief Superintendent Archie Bishop came back from the woods, which he did as soon as he received Inspector Rosher's radio call, he took that man with him, up again to the Chief Constable's office, where he, the inspector and the Chief all agreed that this might well be the breakthrough, indeed it might. They agreed it was too much money for a lad to have come by honestly, and that manifestly this lad had not. They agreed that the Nilhildrin even now being applied to the notes might reveal things of great interest. No disagreement crept in at all. The Archbishop said to his satellite: "Suggest you get out there right away, Mr. Rosher, before they change their minds." Himself, he would stay here, hovering over the Forensic Department and putting the lens over whatever came out of it.

"Uh-huh," said Rosher, knowing full well what his leader meant. It happens often that parents, having alerted the police regarding sibling activity, repent before the police arrive and destroy or remove the evidence. Mothers in particular do it. He left at once, pausing only to summon Detective Sergeant Panton from his desk. On a job involving entry to a home and search of it or part thereof, it is dangerous to go alone.

The remarkable weather was holding. They had a pleasant drive out to Hutton Fellows. Not much conversation, Inspector Rosher was not a man given to much nattering; but the sergeant did say as they swept through the green and gold countryside:

"Saw the girl last night. The Watson-Harvey girl. She was with the Wellington lads, in the Laughing Jackass. They reckon she's a right raver."

"Who do?"

"My grass. I was there on business." He put that in because it is well not to have a superior think you took off while on call for a murder case, to jump up and down in a disco. "Reckons she's well known for it, anybody can have her. Wouldn't think so, would you, to look at her?"

"We're on a murder job, lad," Inspector Rosher told him, "not an investigation into morals. What she does with it's her business."

"Yes," said Sergeant Panton, snubbed again. "Mm. I just thought—you know. Coincidence, seeing them there." He lapsed into silence while the car ran through the lanes, over the bridge, into the village and on to the Poddys' house, where Inspector Rosher arranged his face while he waited on the doorstep.

Mrs. Poddy showed them up to her dead son's bedroom. A very neat and rigourously tended room—sectarian women are fanatically opposed to dust and bits of fluff under the beds. By their creed, spotlessness is next to Godliness and half a lap ahead—though ordinary enough in its furnishing. There was no sign of hobby or interest normal in bedrooms belonging to the young. Just a bed, a dressing table, a wardrobe, a wicker chair, all personality scrubbed and polished away. The floor was of bare and highly polished boards, just one rug set beside the bed. Rosher glanced around at it as he moved in. Floors are always of interest to a detective, it is remarkable what lies under them. He'd have all those boards up; but none of the fastenings that he could see appeared to have been disturbed. Extracting nails and replacing them would leave marks on the softwood surface.

He moved to the wardrobe. Two suits, very sober. Several shirts, shoes, ties, the usual bits and pieces, all neat and the suits in plastic bags. On to the bed. "We'll just have the mattress off, Mrs. Poddy, if you don't mind," he said. Actively engaged, he tended to forget the telephone manner. "Give us a hand, sergeant.

72

Did your son receive a lot of mail, madam?" The money reached him by some means.

"No. None. Except from the hospital. When he was due to—attend."

"Uh-huh." Well, it wouldn't come through the post. He'd collect it from somebody. But mail can point to the somebody. Not often, because criminals prefer not to commit their thoughts to paper; but leave no stone unturned. The small suitcase in which the money had been found was already down in the hall, ready for transporting to the station.

There was nothing funny about the bed or the floor beneath. Nothing about the wicker chair to raise an eyebrow, and only a comb and immaculate hair-brushes on the dressing table. But in one of the drawers lay a writing pad, together with a packet of envelopes and a ballpoint pen. By angling the pad against the window light and squinting along it, the inspector could see the slight indentation left when somebody writes with a ballpoint pen on the sheet above. Now this sort of thing is often very useful indeed, the Forensic boys can do wonders with it. "We'll take this along with us, Madam," he said. "The sergeant will give you a receipt. You'll get it back, of course. And perhaps we'd better just have the floorboards up."

"The floorboards?" said Mrs. Poddy.

"Purely routine, madam, in cases of this nature."

The search under the floor yielded nothing but a little sweat from humping the furniture about. They marked the boards slightly, with no objection from Mrs. Poddy, who perhaps welcomed the need for more devout and therapeutic polishing, down upon the knees; but this apart, the room when they left it looked as immaculate as when they arrived. Mr. Poddy, who had stayed in the living room throughout, appeared when they descended again to the hall. "Is everything all right?" he asked.

"It seems to be, sir, yes," said Inspector Rosher. "We're just borrowing your son's writing materials. Make the receipt out, sergeant."

By the time they were back in the car it was very nearly two o'clock, and the inspector still had not lunched. Half-an-hour's drive lay before him, and the chance existed that a sudden blow-up in this or some other case would rob his solid frame of necessary nourishment, if he did not push something between his big brown teeth now. Well, the pubs were still open and the radio would have squawked if he was needed back in the town. Easing the car out onto the road, he said to Sergeant Panton: "Raise the station. Tell 'em if we're not needed, you're taking me for a pie."

There are two pubs in Hutton Fellows, both on the through road, both ancient and both attractive. One is too smartly thatched and has been tarted somewhat with Georgian-style bay windows and a lunch-and-grill room, for the benefit of the tourist. The other is also thatched, but more shaggily. It has two low-beamed bars, one with the old oak settles. This is where the locals go. This is where Rosher went, because the landlady's home-baked pies are famous, and much cheaper than the plastic pork in cardboard crust that comes wrapped in plastic at the other place, with a garnish of limp cress.

The beer is good, too, at the smaller place. It is a free house, and the landlord is a connoisseur who conducts frequent deep-probing quality tests and has the nose and belly to prove it. His wife would have him smarten up a bit, tart the place a little to attract the tourist trade like them down the road, or at least not freeze the little ole buggers out when they do wander in. He tells her to get stuffed. Now he stood in soiled shirtsleeves behind a counter enriched with the patina of three centuries of spilled beer and nodded warily to the policemen as they came in.

"'Afternoon," said Rosher; and to Sergeant Panton: "I'll have a pint. Bitter."

"Ah," the sergeant said. "Yes." First man through the door usually says what'll you have. The inspector was first through the door. "Er, a pint of bitter, please. And . . . er, another pint. Two pints."

"Two pints each?" the landlord said.

"No, just two pints."

"Might as well get a couple of pies, while you're at it," said Rosher.

"I've eaten. Had lunch before we came out."

"I didn't."

"Ah. Er—and a pie, please."

"One's no good, two bites and it's gone. Better leave it at two."

"Ah. Yes. Two pies, please."

The landlord was at the good old-fashioned beer-pull. "Two pints of bitter and—how many pies?"

"Two." Christ!

The landlord knew Rosher. He'd been in Hutton Fellows before, notably at the time when Mr. Henry Croker, a well-respected pillar, tried to fly too high and came unstuck. He drew the beer, brought the pies and said in the voice of well-crusted malt loaf: "You here about the murder, or the sheep-savaging?"

Sergeant Panton was counting out his money. Inspector Rosher said: "What sheep-savaging?"

"Up the Wellingtons." Shouted loud, it could have been a football cry. "Lorst five, larse night. Didden they tell you?" He nodded to a wizened small customer sucking in beer between the gums. Old Ossie Horrick enjoying his fiver, sitting on one of the fireside settles. "He found 'em."

Rosher lifted his pint, said "cheers," took a swig that left white foam on his upper lip, bit into a pie and looked at the aged man. Old Ossie was talking, to a character who looked almost as old but was, in fact, his son, Young Ossie. "So there they be, all dead. So I says shall I notify police, and they say no, they says, they'll deal with ut, they says. We'll deal with ut, they say, and they gives me a fiver."

"Doan go fur nowadays," said his son. "Doan go fur, a fiver don't. Not nowadays."

"Arr," his father said. "Arr—you'm right there. I can remember when ut were a penny a pint. And now they buried 'un, seed 'em doing ut. Didn't notify nobody, did they?"

It is not usual for countrymen to babble in front of any old body, especially strangers and most especially policemen. Young Ossie, true to his roots, was shifting his eyes sideways when he tried awkwardly to head his father toward generalities; but Old Ossie, deaf and grown garrulous with the onset of senility, sitting with his back to the bar was not even aware of policemen. He was gone, anyway, beyond the stage of inverted suspicious caution to where a man will gabble eagerly of any matter which colours the terrible monotony of his declining years with a hint of drama. So he went on: "They haven't notified young Ted Phillis, that I do know. If they had, he'd have come over, wooden 'ee? He'd have come to have a look at 'em. How they gooing to claim insurance if 'ee ayn had a look at 'em?"

"How about another pint?" his son suggested, eyes still inclined to wabble toward the policemen at the bar.

"Doan moind if I do," Old Ossie said. Even the senile, if his ancestry be peasant back to the roaring days of William the Conqueror and beyond, even to Egbert and Eggwhite and Eggfroth and all the visiting Vikings, picks up signals in the end. He glanced behind him; found the policemen, and promptly clammed up. You could see him do it. When his gnarly old offspring fetched new pints, making a grudging "Arternoon" as he stood beside the big men to collect, they embarked upon the slow sinking of them in silence.

Now a policeman engaged upon a murder inquiry does not yearn to add to the workload anything so commonplace as sheep-savaging, reported or unreported. If law has been breached, it is up to the local bobby to do something about it. But: A policeman engaged upon a murder inquiry is cogitating, and evaluating a limited number of people. People whose lives touched upon the life lately destroyed. Unorthodox behaviour by one or some of these people is among the things he hopes for. If it be irrational enough, it can change the status of the party from walk-on to suspect.

Here was unorthodox behaviour. Sheep slaughtered—good sheep, the lads said they were breeding for prizes—and buried quietly with the police apparently not notified. Ted Phillis, the old man said. P.C. Ted Phillis, Rosher knew him. Saw him last at the

76

scene of the murder. Even if he had been notified and had seen the sheep: shouldn't the carcases have been left above ground until somebody from the insurance called? Sheep are expensive commodities. Hmm.

The inspector stood and demolished both excellent pies, thinking as his brown teeth rotated. The landlord, too, had his share of countryman's taciturnity, except when somebody mentioned beer. And Sergeant Panton was thinking: Am I paying for his bloody lunch, then? And he fiddles it on his expenses? Sod that. So silence reigned in the bar.

When he had drained his pint, Rosher said: "Ah. That's better. Very salubrious. I'd buy you another, but I don't want you getting breathalised. 'Afternoon, landlord." And he bandied to the door. Sergeant Panton hastily swallowed the last of his beer before he followed. If he wasn't getting another, he wasn't bloody well leaving this.

Outside, the inspector said: "Remind me I owe you one. And if they don't need me back at the station, we'll pay a little call." There was no great rush to have the dead lad's writing pad dipped into something, or possibly powdered over. Follow the new little thing while you are adjacent is the golden rule. They will flog the soles of your feet for sure, if it turns out later that you should have done and didn't.

He spoke on the car radio to the station. No movement in the big case, and no report of sheep-savaging, at Hutton Fellows or elsewhere. P.C. Phillis had made his daily contact call, and said nothing about it. "Better get hold of him," the inspector said. "The Wellington place. I'm looking in before I come back." Don't mention me, the sergeant thought. I'm not here, am I? Until it comes to paying for the bloody grub. "Over and out," said Inspector Rosher.

It was, of course, and still is, not far from the village to the farm. On any fine bank holiday you can walk it quicker than you can get there by car. Today was not a bank holiday. Rosher pointed the bonnet that way and in a very few minutes was turning it into the drive and on to the yard looked into by French windows and the front door. He got out. Sergeant Panton got out. They went to the door. Inspector Rosher rang the bell. Once—a wait. Twice—a wait. Three times—and a wait. "Nobody in," he said, bending his body to peer through the letter box.

The door opened. Hee hee hee, went Sergeant Panton inwardly. The inspector came upright. "Ah," he said. "Good afternoon, madam." Blessed though he was with a very thick skin, he spoke abruptly; sternly, forgetting entirely to switch on his telephone voice, and the act of snatching off the hat came belatedly. A touch disconcerting, to be found by a female public bent to navel height and peering through her letter box.

But the lady would not have noticed. Her hair was a mess, her moist eyes creased with the effort of finding focus. Head wobbling slightly on a thin and ravaged neck she held on to the edge of the door and said: "Yes? Yes? Who is it?"

"Detective Inspector Rosher, madam. I was hoping for a word with your sons." The accent was functioning now, the brown teeth were bared in the beam.

Mrs. Wellington shifted her grip to the jamb and threw the door wide. "Come in," she said. "Come in. Whoops!" The last, because but for a sudden clutch she would have fallen out, flat upon the doorstep.

"Ah," said Inspector Rosher. "Thank you. Most kind."

He led his sergeant through the door, and Mrs. Wellington preceded them at a rapid totter across the sullen hall and into the glum living room. There she stopped, turned, teetered, looked at them, and said: "Who did you say?"

"Detective Inspector Rosher, madam. May one suggest that you sit down?"

"Ah," she said. "Yes. Yes. Yes, I think I might. You were here before."

"That's right," the inspector said. He was dropping the telephone manner, but retaining the benevolence. "Sergeant, help the lady to her chair."

The sergeant moved forward. The lady drew herself up. "I am quite calpable, thank you," she said, and attained the chair under her own power. A bottle stood on the table beside it, together with a glass. "Would you care for a little dwinkie?" she asked.

"Thank you, madam, no. I was hoping to see your sons."

"Out," she said. "Such good boys, I'd like to introjoose you to them, but out. Business affairs."

"Ah. And what business affairs would that be?" Pump when you can. Who knows what may come of it?

"Business? What business?"

"You said they're out on business."

"Yes. Yes. Out on business."

"Do you know what time they'll be back?"

The twins answered this for themselves, by arriving. The door opened and they came in; not flustered, exactly, but showing signs of having hurried. As indeed they might. They were emerging from the wood fringing the property with shot-guns and a dead rabbit when they saw the inspector arriving. "Christ," said Simon, "we don't want him poking about with only the old trout in the house." Down they came at the half run; and here they were, guns and rabbit and all.

"Ah," said the inspector. "Good afternoon." The benevolence, fading during the abortive conversation with the mother, vanished entirely when he addressed her sons. They could be malefactors, if only in the minor matter of failing to report savage sheep.

"Good afternoon," Simon said. Smiling, and very pleasant. "What brings you back, Mr. . . . er, Rosher?"

The inspector indicated Timothy's gun. It was pointed straight at his belly. "I hope that thing's not loaded," he said.

"Sorry." Timothy shifted the aim. "Nothing in it."

"It's about your sheep, sir." Rosher was addressing Simon. Something subtle in the ambience surrounding them suggested that he was the dominant partner.

"Oh yes?"

"I believe you had some savaged. Killed."

"That's right, five of them."

"Didn't it occur to you that we should be notified?"

"You weren't here." A pleasant smile; but almost mocking.

Don't come funny with me, you young bugger. "The police. You have a local man."

"Old Ted Phillis, yes. The boy with the bicycle clips."

Saucier yet. And untrue, Constable Phillis drove a neat little Mini van. Both twins were grinning now. The inspector injected a touch of Old Blubbergut bark into his voice. "Don't you know the police should be notified?"

His tone played upon the twin's innate arrogance as bagpipes upon the sufferer with earache. Chin risen, Simon said: "Why?"

He's going to put his foot in his mouth, the sergeant thought. The sods are setting him up. "Not by law, sir," Panton said to Simon, quietly. "The law was changed, as you know and we know, very recently." That should be hint enough.

Inspector Rosher, grim faced—oh, he knew when clever little fellows were sending him up. He knew—he knew; and he marked them down—daggered his acolyte with hard little eyes. "I was calling attention to the moral aspect, sir. Dangerous dog loose— surely you felt it your duty to spread the word among your fellow farmers?"

No black mark, for a policeman not to know the changing of an obscure law. Town policemen like Rosher meet few cases of sheep-worrying, they are handled by the country copper; but no policeman may display ignorance of any law, and seasoned ones hide such ignorance very quickly.

The twins were not fooled, their eyes said so. Simon replied. "We're spreading the word. We've just been out doing it."

Rosher carried on with the reangling that deceived nobody. "A call to your constable would have relieved you of the need. He has better facilities, surely." A Mini van, and a beat easily adapted to visiting all the farms in the area.

"If you think we need special facilities, Mr.—er—Rosher, you don't know villages. There won't be a farm for miles around that doesn't know about it by this time." An edge of amused contempt now under the young man's voice.

"And what about the insurance position?" Companies won't

pay out on a heap of patted-down earth. They'll demand exhumation. Or the word of a copper who saw the sheep before they were buried; as they must be, quickly, for the sake of hygiene.

"That's our business," said Simon, quite witheringly; and Timothy added:

"They're our sheep."

Mrs. Wellington spoke up, from the chair where she sat pouring from bottle to glass. "Sheep. They're our sheep." She lifted her voice suddenly, in quavering song. "All in the A-April e-e-evening, April airs were abro-oard, I saw the sheep with their la-a-ambs—"

Harshly, without attempt at social disguise, Simon said: "Shut up, Mother." The lady subsided. He turned again to Rosher. "If that's all, Inspector—it is Inspector, isn't it?—we're pretty busy."

"Good boys." Their mother took the glass away from her lips to say it. "Such good boys."

"Yes, sir," said the stern gorilla. The knowing bent looked about for cover, when that glitter came into the eyes. "That's all. For now."

"Then I'm sure you will excuse us. We have work to do. Tim, show the inspector out, will you?"

"Goodbye," said Mrs. Wellington, the toothy grin of the gracious hostess suddenly recreasing her destroyed face. "Do come again."

"I wouldn't be at all surprised, madam," said Inspector Rosher. "I wouldn't be at all surprised." Well, at least he had the last word.

When Timothy had ushered them off the premises and closed the door, Sergeant Panton said as they settled into the car: "Poor old Mum. On the way to pink elephants."

"Let's get something straight," barked Inspector Rosher. At this young man he could bark, and a bark he badly needed. "When I'm working on a subject, you keep your mouth shut. If I need your help I'll ask for it."

You silly old sod, the sergeant thought angrily. They were

working on *you*, and you know it. One more step, you'd have looked a right berk. As indeed you are.

They drove on, over the bridge and out of the village; wrapped in fuming silence until the radio spoke. Message for Detective Inspector Rosher. Would he report back to the station, please. No need to set the siren screaming and come zooming through the town, but some of the money was funny.

Timothy said to Simon, when he came back into the living room: "Exit the bold Rosher, with a flea in his ear. I'm just wondering if we should have done it."

"Bloody old nanny goat," said Simon.

"Blurry ole nanny boat," said the mother.

"Not such a fool as he looks, though," Timothy said. "Don't forget the Avenger. And the Croker fellow, just up the road."

"Bloody Avenger. Half-witted sex maniac. We'd better get Mother up to bed again, before she falls off that chair."

When Inspector Rosher reached the station he went straight up, bunched the fist that stretched many a man flat in the days of his lusty youth (and not a few fancying themselves since) and used the hairy knuckles to knock upon the Chief Constable's door. When he entered he found, as they had told him downstairs he would, Chief Superintendent Archie Bishop and Inspector Bennie (Stinkfinger) Clarke from Forensic, standing by while the Chief Constable, seated at his desk, eyed through a magnifying lens one of the notes from the Poddys' small case. The case itself stood upon the desk, and what was obviously the rest of the packet from which the note came, although the sealing band had been removed. The Chief looked up and said: "Ah, Mr. Rosher. There you are."

"Yes, sir," said Rosher; because the Chief had looked down again, squinting into his lens like a camel trying to peep through the eye of a needle. He had to say something. He moved his boxy-toed shoes over the yielding carpet and went to stand beside Superintendent Bishop, who said with ripe dignity: "It's up the stick, that little lot. Funny money."

"Uh-huh," said Inspector Rosher. "Just this packet?"

Inspector Clarke took it upon himself to answer. "The rest's legit. The funnies were at the bottom."

"I've asked my bank manager to come over and confirm," the Chief said. Nice of him, nice of them all, to put the newcomer into the picture. Just shows what courtesy from the top man will do. So long as he is present. "Not that there's much doubt. Very good. Very good. But on the real fiver, the black line is closer to the Queen's head. And the water mark is not quite right." He pushed aside his lens and rubbed the eye he had been using. "Five hundred poundsworth, and it'll all have to go to Scotland Yard. Pity, one could just do with five hundred pounds. Tax free."

He smiled, to make sure everybody realised that he was making a joke. His loyal men smiled back, to assure him that they had no doubt of it. Rosher said: "Dabs on 'em?"

Bennie Clarke answered again. "Only the ones you'd expect, the lad who put them in the case."

"Uh-huh," said Rosher. Paucity of prints was to be expected. If these were good forgeries, as the Chief said they were, whoever produced and handled them would know enough not to send them out with dabs all over.

"Plenty on the legit stuff," Inspector Clarke said. "The fingerprint lads are working on 'em now. Not that it will do us much good, I reckon."

Again, Rosher knew what he meant. Any good policeman would. These were mostly used notes, there would be traces left by previous circulation. There would be marks left by tellers, counting them over, amid the mix of stains and blemishes accumulated from pub counters and store tills and all the likely and unlikely places where bank notes are passed. Unless luck gave them a clear dab matched in the police files, no agency under God could trace that lot out. No way. No way.

"What about you, Mr. Rosher?" The Chief smiled upon his protege. "Did you have any luck?"

Rosher, as usual, responded to the upper-echelon accent with a touch of his telephone manner. "Not really, sir, no. Gave the room a going-over, found a writing pad with impressions on it—it's with Forensic now. Nothing else."

He did not mention his visit to the Wellington farm, or the unorthodoxy that sent him. For one thing, sheep-savaging is not the business of a man sent to investigate murder, unless it has bearing. Secondly: he had not been able as yet to check the law relating to it, so any questioning here could be awkward. Better button the lip. Perhaps because his subconscious mind clicked into gear to divert attention from Hutton Fellows, or perhaps he was a good policeman and had a good idea from time to time, he had one now. "We may be able to get a trace through a bank, sir. Find out whose account the legit came from."

"Mm?" the Chief looked up at him, expectantly.

"Most traceable prints ought to be from bank clerks. They hold 'em down firmly while they count them out. And a firm hold leaves the best prints."

"We can't legally fingerprint all the bank clerks in the country, though, can we?" No reproof in the Chief's manner. Gentle encouragement, rather. He knew his clever lad had more to say than this. But it was the Archbishop who carried the matter forward.

"We can send men in to make withdrawals from their accounts, though. Those who haven't got 'em can start one, or something. Anything that brought forth documents or notes handled by the counter staff. If we draw blank in our own area, no doubt other forces will cooperate. We do need to know where this money came from."

No need to cross every τ, for a good policeman. Archie Bishop made his speech with a nod of approval, knowing the inspector had the idea complete in his mind.

And it was a neat idea. By law, the police cannot fingerprint except after definite arrest. They can ask for cooperation, where a search must be narrowed, but this is not to say they will get it. Many people object strenuously, believing the resultant dabs will go into a malignant secret file, to be used against them at some future date. One or two objecting stridently enough—and there are

84

always some vociferously antagonistic to the police—can lead to questions in Parliament, and leading articles beyond the tit page in the Daily Sun headlined ARE WE A POLICE STATE?

So Rosher's idea was a little Lulu, allowing unobtrusive skirting of the law; and truth is, the police could not function if they did not skirt when necessary. None of those printed would ever know it was done. Not even the ones, if such turned up, who paid out the money, if it came from an account, and were spoken to politely. The Chief Constable might well say, "Well done, Mr. Rosher."

"Thank you, sir," said Rosher.

"Will you see to it, Mr. Bishop?"

And so it came about that many police officers withdrew bits of their savings, all over the town, and later put them back in. Or, in the case of those to whom the feel of it in the fist is fatal, blued it. Others started accounts, destined to be closed down again almost immediately. No guarantee that the stunt would work, of course. Whoever paid all that money out may have drawn it a stash somewhere, nowhere near a bank. Still, it gave a lot of people something to do.

One more matter of interest rounded off the day. The pad came from Forensic, with the writing on the indented page now crystal clear. It said:

Beloved Daddy-Bunny,
The last lot was not where it should be. If it is not there tomorrow I am coming to see what is happening.

> Luv and kisses.
> Your own.

"Queer?" said the Archbishop. "Some kind of blackmail?"

"Could be," said Rosher. They were alone in the super's office.

"Nobody has hinted that he was homo? His parents—anybody?"

"No. Well, his parents wouldn't. Wouldn't even recognise it, would they? If they did they wouldn't admit it. And he might not have been."

"Daddy-Bunny. Luv and kisses. Your Own. Highly suspect."

"Bit too much. Could be sort of a piss-take."

"You cannot," the Archbishop pontificated, "take the piss without handling the member. No smoke without fire. Or, to paraphrase: no piss without steam. Ha ha ha. That's rather good. I think we'd better take it over, see if his parents can help us."

"I'll get out there again," said Rosher. "Have I got time for a cup of tea?" How much more amenable he was, how much more useful, when teamed with anybody other than Chief Superintendent (Percy) Fillimore. In harness with Archie Bishop, he even seemed willing to function as horse behind.

"No, no, I'll go," the super said. "Time I introduced myself. You carry on here." He did not say with what; and this indicates why Rosher worked easily with him. He respected every man's professional competence. Percy would have issued orders. Unnecessary ones that amounted, in Rosher's eyes, to insult.

So it was Archie Bishop who called upon the Poddys this time, to show them a photostat copy of their son's brief letter and to ask gentle questions. The implication that their dead lamb was queer as a cuckoo, or at least consorting queerly, seemed to pass them by. They knew, they said, of nobody to whom he would write in such strange terms. They knew of no men, or older men, with whom he was or had been particularly close.

In fact, as Inspector Rosher had done earlier, Superintendent Bishop came away thinking that they appeared to know very little about their son's private life, whatever.

9

That night, the weather broke. A gale that was more than a gale came screaming malevolent down from the north; clouting down chimneypots one of which, in the town, hit one of the few beat policemen and jammed the helmet over his eyes; tearing the gold and russet leaves from the trees, leaving them shocked and naked in deluging rain wondering what the hell had happened. Worst storm since records began, the papers said next day. Millions of poundsworth of damage and an old lady in Exeter drowned in her very own cellar, trying to stem the flood with a sponge, a mop and a bucket.

At Hutton Fellows the river rose, unable to cope. Flash-water rushing to it from the surrounding hills, meeting water already rejected, backed up in confusion to cover the entire valley. Not very deeply, not so deeply as in 1928, when people sculled up and down in boats plucking people off the thatch; but deeply enough, so that only the half-submerged bridge and garden fences and the lie of the pretty houses told where the streets lay; and almost without exception the cellars and lower floor rooms of those houses were flooded, to some degree.

The two pubs got it. The larger, with its stock all in metal barrels, did not bother much; but the landlord of the other severely aggravated his hernia, sobbing up his precious casks to the ground floor. Silly old sod, his wife said, standing by in her curlers. Now perhaps he'd accept the brewery offer and have it in metal can-nisters fizzed out by electric, like them up the road. And at three o'clock she went back to bed, leaving him to get on with it. The insurance was all paid up, on the house policy and on him.

Old Ossie got it, but didn't know until morning. He lay snoring gleefully in the deep sleep that comes after investing a fiver in jolly good ale. The Poddys got it, and Mrs. Poddy was the only person in the village glad to receive it. A God-fearing woman assuages grief on her knees; and here was muck for a week. All the people in the valley got it, including the Wellingtons, whose farm, although it is well out of the village, sits low in a fold of the hills. But the bigger houses around stand higher, so that the Watson-Harveys escaped. And out from a cavity in the bank bordering a seldom frequented sunken lane a mile away, when the rising water caused newly dug leaf-and-bracken camouflaged earth to collapse, another body came gently floating, face turned up to the dirty black, swag-bellied sky.

At ten o'clock the following morning, they held the inquest on young Poddy. His parents splashed up out of the valley for it—the rain stopped for a few hours from around dawn, which gave the river a chance. Cars could get in and out by nine o'clock—and the whole glum business was over by ten-thirty. The obvious verdict: Murder by person or persons unknown; and permission given for the burying of all that remained from furtive conception in a dark room and the years of pitiful love and sacrifice and stress that had shaped his life and theirs ever since. All gone.

Detective Chief Superintendent Bishop and Detective Inspector Rosher had a word with the parents before they left for the silent house where Mrs. Poddy, tears streaming, would attack with desperate zeal all that mud and sludge while her husband sat stiff in his chair, reading the big black Bible. They—the detectives—had turned away from the press, who were here in fair numbers, and walked over the old tiles to the handsome doorway. A good building, the courthouse. Georgian, with wide steps up to the portico. Ionic columns, very good.

The Poddys stood here, hesitating perhaps because of the renewed rain before descending to their prim, black and aging car; pale, stressed faces, sober in oddly old-fashioned black clothing (perhaps there is a sort of sectarian Moss Brothers, who supply such things for funeral occasions), and stiff with defensive hostility. The superintendent, whose archbishopness fitted him beautifully into all funerals, inquests, assaults upon choirboys, Tom Peeping, popping out naked at nunneries (Big City actually borrowed him once, to investigate the latter) and the like, spoke deeply:

"Ah—Mrs. Poddy—Mr. Poddy—good morning. Saw you inside, of course, but there was no chance to speak. A sad occasion, a very sad occasion."

Without acknowledging his greetings, they looked at him and at Rosher standing beside him. Mrs. Poddy said abruptly: "Are you doing anything about—it?"

"There are developments, madam," the Archbishop told her soothingly. "We are all working very hard, you may be sure. I believe you know Detective Inspector Rosher."

Rosher they knew better than than they knew him, whose one short meeting with them took place yesterday. Nevertheless, they ignored the introduction. They looked out at the grey rain falling out of a grey sky onto a town gone pewter-grey; but they did not move on to their car, so presumably they expected more speech and were prepared to receive it. Rosher supplied a little.

"I was out at your sister's place yesterday, Mrs. Poddy. After I saw you. Some of their sheep had been savaged, perhaps she told you." When she wasn't speechless. She hadn't turned up this morning, had she? Nor had the sons?

Mrs. Poddy's sharp hardness grew harder yet. "We do not correspond with my sister. Her ways are not our ways."

"Ah. I thought the lads—"

Bleakly she turned her head away, lips closed in that thin line. Mr. Poddy said: "We don't have much to do with them. They led . . . our boy . . . into . . . sinful ways."

"Uh-huh. What ways would they be?"

"The ways of the Devil, Mr. Rosher. The ways that lead to perdition. Good morning."

They moved off; descended the steps and got into the car. The two policemen stood, one in a good tweed overcoat worn with a soft felt hat, the other black-hatted as ever above the battleship-grey raincoat, watching them go. The superintendent did not mention that this was the first he had heard of Rosher's visit to the Wellingtons. If he went, he had his reasons. He said: "Poor people. Not much joy in that sort of religion, is there? Not much comfort." He sounded like Dr. Runcie, kicking off the Sunday mishmash on Radio Two. "Well, we'd better get back to the station."

This they did; and were no sooner there than they were off again, gone behind slurping windscreen wipers to view that other body, floated out from its shallow grave. While they were on the way, the twins discovered the water in their cellar.

They could have found it long ago, and the reason why they did not is simple: it had never happened before, in their lifetime. The great inundation of 1928 put three feet of water down there, as it flooded the entire valley; but in 1928 they were not even a rising in the area of their long-dead father's old-fashioned button fly, itself many years from supersedence by the erratic and highly dangerous zip. When they got up, early as sheep farmers must do to check the stock after a roaring night, there was no hint on the living-room level of water below, and because the stone-setted yard drained quickly into the lower ground, although it bounced with rain and was mucky with leaves and mud, it was not flooded. Nor were their fields, standing above the level of the lane.

They moved the sheep to the higher ground at the back of the meadow and penned them there, because sheep are such fools they will wander down again; and with the rain threatening to end its morning break, went back to the house to cook their own breakfast. Mrs. Wellington was still groaning in the bed in which she spent more and more of her time. No use expecting her to come up with something tasty.

Well, they were used to that. They made a far better fist at self-catering than Inspector Rosher ever managed, in his increasingly cluttered and dusty house on the hill. Eggs, bacon, coffee, even toast with marmalade; and still it did not occur to them to check the cellar.

They did this after various jobs about the barns, when they came in again for a coffee break with the rain now teeming. Even now, when he went down Timothy was not inspecting for water. He went to fetch up three £500 packets of the funny money. In the highest traditions of the Post Office, the mail had gone through, old Lennie Fosset splashing up the drive while they were out about the barns. So they found just now, lying on the mat, the very ordinary typed letter from a man who signed himself squiggle; a few paragraphs referring to sheep dip that told them the time was ripe to spread another load. A bit late arriving, but what the heck. They were lucky to get it at all. You try riding a bicycle with a sack on the shoulder and water up to the very hub-caps.

He went, young Timothy, to the cellarhead that leads off from the kitchen and halfway down to where the light switch was. When he snipped it he saw the water, covering the floor. "Oh, Christ," he said, and came up again. Called to Simon, who was shoving the cleaner up and down over the living room carpet. They were not bad housekeepers, by now. Not bad at all. Did it all themselves, rather than have a woman in. A woman will gossip about the drinking habits of another woman, and village women like to pry beadily into larders, into bedrooms, into cellars. . . ."It's flooded."

"What is?" Simon asked.

"The bloody cellar. It's flooded."

Simon echoed that first involuntary exclamation. "Oh, Christ." He dropped what he was doing and came running. It's a big house, you can work up a reasonable lick. Significant, that Timothy stood aside so that his brother went first into the cellar. Mind you, he was not far behind.

The flood could not be called serious. About an inch of water, no more; but the funny money was in a cardboard box labelled as a preparation necessary for sheep farming, together with another containing the drug stock, hidden beneath a couple of similar boxes which did contain the preparation behind a pile of cellar-junk.

They splashed to the corner, not even kicking off the slippers donned whenever they entered the house. The man who must do his own housework soon learns how loathsome is mud, left all over the place by wellie boots. Shoving aside the concealing clutter they picked up the two cardboard boxes, hands beneath to keep the soaked bottoms from collapse, and carried them up the stairs.

They put the boxes down on the kitchen table. The cocaine, coming to them in powder form enclosed in a plastic bag, should have been all right; but water had seeped through the opened and refolded top of the bag, so that many thousands of pounds sterling were converted to a semi-liquid blanc mange. The top four packets of funny money escaped, apart from dampness at the base; but the bottom four were saturated. Polythene between the two layers had minimised damage to the packets above.

Now the basic savagery in these lads showed plain enough as they bent over their ruined goods. Timothy snarled: "Bastard! Bastard! What're we going to do?"

Simon, as savage, said: "Deliver what we can today. Report what happened and tell them we'll get the rest away when we've dried 'em out."

"That's the money. What about this?" Timothy indicated the other mess. The one that represented investment of virtually all of their capital. "Can you dry junk out?"

"We can bloody well try."

"Gas stove? In the oven?" Many things can be dried that way.

"Not here, not with Mother poking about."

"She's too far gone to notice if we shoved her in with it."

"No, I'm not," said Mother, from the doorway. She was up, and half cut already. Perhaps it was the lingering from last night. Although, of course, she had her bottle in her room.

Simon whirled. "Sod off!" he roared. "Go on, fuck off!" And Timothy was saying, as murderous in attack: "Get out, you old cow, get out! Get back to your room!"

Obediently the mother turned, paused for a moment to assist balance with a hand on the doorjamb, and half-weaved away; tears suddenly brimming the streaked, out-of-focus eyes; murmuring her incantation. "Good boys. Such good boys. . . ."

The lads stood in raging silence until she was well on her way up the stairs. Then Timothy said: "Do you think she knows what she was looking at?"

"No. We'll have a word with her later, tell her she'd better not. Get a bottle in her and a couple of pills, she'll forget all about it anyway."

"Bloody liquor's becoming an expense."

"Won't be for long. You have to speculate to accumulate, if we kept her sober we couldn't do it our way.

"So where are we going to put this stuff? Upstairs?"

"No. No need to tempt fate—she might come across it, and that bloody Rosher got in yesterday while our backs were turned. We'll stash it in the barn."

"What about drying 'em?"

"Not the oven—it might be too dry. Might do something to the paper." Change the feel—make it brittle—fade the ink—only an expert would know. Simon was no expert; but you take no chances with £2,000 worth of notes, face value. "We can use the truck engine cover."

This was a fair idea. The engine of the enclosed truck was situated between the driver and the passenger seats, well back in the cab. The big cover was very useful for drying wet clothing on. It formed a handy radiator when the engine was warm. Add a butane gas heater in the body of the truck—they had a couple, to make winter work in the barns endurable—and you could spread the notes around in an atmosphere less drastically parched than the inside of an electric oven. Hang them up to drain away the worst of it; spread them, twenty, thirty, maybe fifty—one full packet— at a time on the cover to finish them off under the eye, fingering to gauge progress so that nothing dried out too far. If you needed to leave it all, you locked the truck up. Not that you would leave it; but it was innocuous-looking privacy within the innocuous privacy of the barn. You could supervise, if you wished, from the yard. Anybody approaching, simply nip in and turn the engine off.

No need for Simon to explain all this to Timothy. Even had the almost telepathic rapport not been working, he'd dried wet shirts and things on the engine cover. When they did a little smalls-washing they often timed it to chime in with a necessary journey in the truck. So now he simply picked up the funny money box, very carefully, and made for the door, where he paused, as did Simon coming behind with the box of slushy cocaine, to kick off his slippers and don the rubber boots standing there. Pointless, in a way, because slippers and socks were saturated. But a farmer going out into rain will put on his wellies automatically, especially when abstracted.

An hour later, tests had proved that the system worked very satisfactorily: they pinned the notes to sheets of plywood and stood them in front of the portable heater to extract the main moisture; then they started the engine and so warmed the cover to finish them off. The condensation, they felt, was all to the good. Simon said, "I'll take this first lot, then. Better keep them in complete batches. I'd better get off. Back in an hour or so."

They had rearranged the morning to fit the situation. Instead of going together to the rendezvous point near the big city where they would be handed over to the actual distributors, Simon would now go alone, Timothy staying to carry on with the drying process. So with the dry notes and the single packet of restored ones completed so far—they looked all right, felt all right—Simon took off in the car; by which time Superintendent Bishop and Inspector Rosher, no more than a mile away, were standing in the rain where the body came to rest, discussing the setting up of a Murder Room in the village.

No trouble came to Simon on the drive there and back, and only one incident marred the smoothness of the drying operation. This was when the saturated bottom of the cardboard box fell out as Timothy lifted it from the van floor to place it on a wheel-arch, for easier access. Two packets were still in it. They hit the floor;

and one soaked band burst. There were loose notes now, all around his feet. "Fuck it," he said, and stopped to gather them up.

Three packets, each containing fifty. That is one hundred and fifty notes. No discredit to him, really, that he did not notice until he counted them later that one was missing. He had stepped on it, it stuck to the muddy sole of his wellie boot.

The police doctor had pronounced the body dead of a bashed-in skull and gone. The body was gone, in a canvas bag. The Scenes of Crime men were standing moodily around in the teeming rain, knowing that if anything ever existed such as should be mulled over, it had all been washed away. The photographer had taken his livid snaps and gone, the fingerprint and forensic men were telling each other it was a waste of bloody time turning out, conditions like this. What are we supposed to do? they said. I tell you—sodding waste of time.

The brims of the hats topping Superintendent Bishop and Inspector Rosher dripped cunningly, sorting out the space between neck and upstanding collar. The superintendent said: "There's not much sense in galloping back and forth to town. If the river comes up again and the rain keeps on we couldn't do it anyway. Buzz the station, tell them we're using the village hall. No—tell them to get the mobile out. It's not in use, is it?"

"Not so far as I know," said Rosher. A few yards away, Sergeant Panton was overseeing the roping off of the area where the body was found by a retired shopwalker out taking after-the-storm photos, who thought for a mad moment that it was a wet window-dummy.

"It can be stationed on the green," said the Archbishop. "Handy for everything." He did not say what everything was. It might have been anything.

Be that as it may, he had made the wise decision. To set up a Murder Room calls for hard work, telephone and radio equipment transported, filing cabinets run in and the whole lot run out again afterwards. The Murder Wagon, however, is a marvellous thing, completely self-supporting. You drive up—cogitate in it, test for fingerprints, bloodstains and anything else in it, even make tea and the arrest in it, if arrest you ever make. When you have finished, you lock up and drive away.

The town was very proud of its Murder Wagon, the tiny part of the electorate that knew it had one. When other forces borrowed it—and they often did, on a sort of hire-basis, there being too few jobs in the town itself to keep it gainfully employed—it was narrowly inspected for bumps and dents and scratches artfully polished over, before the driver returning it was allowed to leave.

"Right," said Inspector Rosher. "I'll see to it."

"Yes, do that. Funny how it goes in cycles, isn't it? Don't see a corpse for months on end, and suddenly we get two of 'em in a couple of days." The super shook his head to scatter the pendant drops from his hat-brim and readjusted the collar of his rain-dark coat. "I'll get down to the autopsy, then. You should have the pictures soon. You'll circulate them, of course?" No instruction. No bull-headed order. Merely a mild query, allowing that his subordinate knew very well what to do. And this is right, this is proper. A man does not become an inspector who fumbles on routine.

"Uh-huh," said Rosher; and they walked together to where the Archbishop boarded his car, left along the narrow, sunken lane, while the inspector raised the station on the radio of a squad car, parked nearby with the vehicles belonging to all those specialists rendered impotent (in a professional sense) by the bitterly inconsiderate rain.

Normally, policemen engaged on a murder case are not called upon to shoulder another. That this norm was being side-stepped was due to the obvious fact: two bodies in one small village in so short a space of time suggests a link, and something very funny going on. So funny as to make of that village a subject meriting very close scrutiny. If the double-dying turned out to be fortuitous: no harm done. They could always hand over when the trails divided. But both would have betted (not money, in Rosher's case— maybe a year of his life) that they would not. Vibrations tell a policeman when cases are connected.

The pictures came to hand even before the Murder Wagon arrived. Not bad going, considering that these, for circulation, were not taken until the body got to the town, and then rushed through (warm developer was the photographer's trick) and sent on by motorbike. Rosher already had pictures from the instant-snap camera used to supplement his plate-camera work; but snaps of a body lying mauled where it is found are too gruesome for public consumption and not very useful in establishing identification. The instant-snaps formed reference for policemen only, until the better shots arrived. The new ones showed the corpse plainly dead, but more decorously arranged and in close-up, with a plain sheet background. Much more suitable.

The inspector received them on the green, even as the Murder Wagon eased into the village over the bridge: three shots, four prints of each, still tacky from the forced drying done on a machine basically similar to the cover over the engine of the Wellington boys' truck. Twelve prints. Enough. The uniform men were here, plenty to swell the house-to-house team since those who normally would crawl shoulder-to-shoulder all over the murder area were rendered superfluous by the weather. He passed the prints to Sergeant Panton, standing now at his side. "Get these out," he said, and turned to supervise the positioning of the Murder Wagon. There is limited hard-standing on the green at Hutton Fellows. You look such a load of Keystones, if you sink in and can't get out again.

It did not take long to establish identity. Several people remembered seeing the young man in the village. Once, sometimes twice. None of them could give him a name, but the Poddys did. They had met him briefly at the hospital, introduced by their son as his friend. Tom Nolan, of course.

By the time Simon returned, Timothy had completed the drying and had transported the notes, together with the cocaine, back into the house; where with his mother safely up in her bedroom— she always sank herself, when they shouted at her—he counted them. Not once, but many times. When Simon came in saying "All right?" he said, still at it:

"Yes. Yes, they're all done. But there seems to be one missing."

"Missing?"

"Well—it may not have been there. I mean—there might have been forty-nine in that bundle, he may have sent it one short. It burst—the bottom of the box did—and I had to pick them all up."

"Where?"

"In the van."

"Did you look in the van?"

"Of course I did, for Christ's sake."

"I mean, did you search it?"

"It's not there."

"Even so, we'd better take another look. Mother all right?"

"Not a peep. She'll be well pissed by now."

"Good. We'll leave this lot in the cupboard, then."

"What about this?" Timothy indicated the sloshy cocaine. "It wouldn't dry in the van." He'd tried; but more than engine and gas heater was called for, to evaporate all that water.

"That can go in the oven. We'll have to get it out of the bag, the heat will melt the plastic. Onto a plate, or something. Shove it in as it is, for now, only don't switch on. We'll deal with it when we come back."

They crossed again to the barn, to search the truck and even, although Timothy swore he never left it, the immediate area around. No sign of the missing note.

Simon said, "Fucking nuisance. We don't want it adrift. And we don't want 'em thinking we're picking off the top."

"I don't think it was there," said Timothy. "I don't see how it could have been."

"Didn't step on it, did you? It didn't stick to your foot?"

Timothy lifted his feet one after the other, to inspect the soles of his boots; but no note was there. It had fallen off long ago.

10

That night, the dog Rover went loose again. He had been very restless since he found out about sheep, tending between long quiescent periods in the company of his beloved to whine at doors, even to scratch at them as if wanting to be let out. He padded up and down, softly whimpering.

The fact is, of course, he was riven. Torn between Fiona-worship and the blood-surging, teeth-tingling new hobby. Much of his unrest, no doubt, came from sensing Fiona's unrest; but most of it came with remembering how they ran, crying in terror before him, and the lust to feel his teeth again sinking gloriously into the throat, and hot blood in his mouth.

The Watson-Harveys held a small and intimate bridge party that night. Not really a party, just a foursome. Fivesome, counting Fiona. The guests were a partner in one of Mr. Watson-Harvey's businesses, a small bald man who spent the evening heavy-breathing inwardly for Fiona and her mother both; and his large wife, who fancied only Fiona. A nymphette, her practised inversion said. A little nympho, or I am a Dutchman. A Dutchman she patently was not.

Rover had been a nuisance through dinner. He was being a nuisance now, when the foursome sat around the table cutting and dealing and sorting out the trumps. Mrs. Watson-Harvey said at last: "Fiona darling, I really do think we shall have to put Rover out."

Fiona was not playing. She was, in fact, very edgy herself. Covering it well from everybody but Rover, but nonetheless very disturbed: by the discovery of Tom Nolan, main topic of conversation during dinner; and by the fact of policemen, all over the village, with their great wagon parked on the green. Even the commutor inhabitants were excited by it all, and the children were having a wonderful time.

"I'll take him to the stable, Mummy, shall I?" she said brightly. Like her mother, she did the social-charm bit well, and quite automatically. She knew the dog's restlessness and had considered taking him upstairs while the older generation played cards; for a time that might quiet him down and divert her from her worries. But the stresses were too great in her tonight, pushing Rover's head away when he hinted. And she looked lovely. Radiant and virginal in her expensive frock.

"I think perhaps you should, darling," her mother said.

"Come along, then, Rover," cried Fiona, very girlishly. "Come along, then, silly old boy. See what you've done? You've got yourself banished."

Everybody smiled. I'd banish you, darling, given half a chance, the gentleman guest thought, and his goaty eye flicked back to the mother as she leaned forward to cut the cards, showing the channel between still very beautiful breasts. His lady wife was watching trim ankles and buttocks as Fiona took the dog out through the kitchen door.

He knew he was being banished, and as always it tortured his mind that she could do this to him; but there was a comparable level of different emotion in him tonight, the tug of the new hobby filling him with savage excitement mingled with that guilt. He whimpered as they crossed the yard, knowing already what he was going to do.

Simon and Timothy, arrogant to the point of egomania provided each was there to confirm their joint infallibility, were not troubled by the presence of policemen thick on the ground and the finding of Tom Nolan's body. They were spending the evening

100

very comfortably, Mother in her room where she had been since this morning, cleaning their guns: two small automatics acquired illegally and carried on forgery-passing trips and the weekly drug hand-out with Fiona, because they were mixing with very funny people these days; and the two licensed shotguns. They liked playing with guns, they liked pull-throughs and little oil bottles and all the maintenance paraphernalia.

Not much talk passed between them. It was seldom necessary, they had this deep communication. Thus, both knew the other was thinking as he was: of profit accruing from their quarter-share of the face value of the notes—the producer took a quarter, the controlling gang handling distribution pocketed half—and of further very high profit beginning to repay the investment of virtually every penny they could muster in drugs, when Fiona led them to it. Both ventures were going very well, no danger threatening above the calculated and stimulating necessary risks since they acted decisively to remove it. The coke in the oven seemed to be drying nicely.

Simon had just reassembled his shotgun when the door chime rang, and was using a cartridge to check clearances and so on. Not a practise to please an army instructor, but people do these things in the privacy of the home. The muzzle was pointed at a display cabinet anyway, so had it gone off it would merely have blasted his mother's best china to pieces. And she no longer looked at it, her interest had passed to bottles.

They did, let it be said, glance at each other when the chime came. A house full of naughtiness—a village full of policemen—strange if they had not. But there was no real quivering in them. Simon said, quite casually, "I'll go," and he went to the door, still holding his shotgun. It was Old Ossie.

Aged countrymen are not surprised, when a man appears at his door carrying a shotgun. He means nothing by it, all farmers have guns and they spend time cleaning them. Or they may be just in from shooting at things, or just going out to do it. They may, of course, have shot the wife, but more likely they have not. Old Ossie did not blink. He said, with an air of self-importance:

"'Evening, Mister Simon. Called to see if you'll be wanting me in the morning.'"

"What?" said Simon, his mind not fully caught up. "Oh—yes. Yes, I reckon so."

"Only I'm preddy busy at the moment, need to know wheer I stand, like."

Old Ossie loved storms. There was work to do after them: ditch-clearing, hen-house repairing, cleaning up of yards, generally restoring order. These days he had no full job, and as he grew older and older and even older, fewer farmers used him even for casual labour. Those who did saw it mainly as an act of charity. So he lived meagerly on his old-age pension (and that had cost the State a packet, by now), payment for the odd job his only taste of honey. Cash always came to pocket after storms; and after this one, business was actually brisk. He came to see the Wellingtons because tomorrow was his day for tidying up their yard. He tidied several yards, on a once-weekly basis.

That he continued to do this small job for the twins was due not so much to charity on their part as to the fact that he always had done it. Somebody has to clean a farmyard, and with no other labour employed they simply never saw reason for changing the system. He did the job well, so long as nobody pressed him, and the alternative was to do it themselves. Not worth it, for the few bob involved. And he was harmless, he never came into the house. So the young man said: "Yes. Come as usual. If we don't get another lot in the night."

"We won't," said Old Ossie. Aged countrymen are weatherwise. "It's clearing, look. Might even get another spell of ole St. Martin's summer." Indeed there were rifts in the cloud cover. Brisk drying breeze from the hills, glimpses of a scurrying moon. "What do 'ee think of ole murder, then? Two of 'em, eh? Coppers all over village, young Ted Phillis never 'ad a time like it. Hee hee hee."

"All good, clean fun," said Simon.

Old Ossie's mind was back with the job. He recovered his tooth and reverted to his air of tycoon self-importance. "Only I'm

102

gooing 'round seeing who wants what doing. Come to see you so I'd know how to fit everybody in, you being one of my reglars, like." He broke off, and his scaly eye sharpened. "What's that?" he said.

"What's what?"

"Gooing into your ole field, look."

Less engaged, Rover would have known they were there. The entrance to the field is no more than thirty, forty yards away. But the sheep were obsessing him now, the breeze that brought the gut-knotting wool-stink to his quivering nostrils blowing away from him any intermingling of human stink. He slipped into the field and slowly, slowly, to prolong the savage joy, advanced belly down toward where he knew the source of the stink was, penned at the top end behind low stone walls. Uncemented dry-stone, rock on rock. Simon leaned his body backward to call through the open door.

"Tim—the dog. Bring some cartridges."

They could move when they wanted to, those boys. By the time Simon reached the wall rimming the field, at a spot much higher and nearer the pen than if he had made for the gate, Timothy was almost beside him with his own gun, loaded as he ran. Yards back Old Ossie hobbled, his wicked old heart a-chortle. It was all happening—cash-money—murder—killer dogs—no end to the filling of his battered old cup, even to running over.

Timothy slipped his brother a cartridge when he came up with him at the wall, and made to level his gun. Simon hissed as he quickly broke barrel from stock and loaded his second chamber: "Not yet—not yet—wait 'til he leaps."

Good thinking. The dog's crouched outline was indistinct against the dark ground. It would not be too clear when he rose up; but they'd hit him all right, with aim taken in advance. He'd go for where the wall was lowest—there, where a few top-layer rocks were missing.

Man, of course, retains his position only by keeping a thought ahead of the animal world. Sure enough, Rover crept straight toward that lower part of the wall, and when he was close he growled menacingly; because something was missing from the game, the mad-blooded, bad, guilty and glorious game. Thus far the sheep had not panicked, and vital to the joy was to have them milling, bleating, running blind in terror. They panicked now, hearing him, their silly blood knowing him for a wolf; and he lept with a wolf-snarl at the wall.

The two guns bellowed almost together. The leaping body twisted in mid-air; flopped back to earth, writhed there with the snarl turned to a scream of pain. "Got the bastard!" crowed Simon, exultant in killing as his brother was, and as the dog had been. "Got him!" Together, the twins went nimbly over the wall. Old Ossie lifted a leg somehow, and came on behind.

The dog glared up at them through his agony when they stood over him. He'd never liked them, he was shut away when they were secret with the beloved, but he knew very well what they were up to. He'd often longed to sink his teeth into their tender parts. Now he snarled. Choked back his creaming agony and snarled. There is spine in a dog that dies snarling.

"Oh, Jesus Christ!" said Timothy.

"Fuck it, fuck it, fuck it," said Simon.

"Oo," said Old Ossie, "ayn that Miss Fiona's dog? Oo—she'm gonna be cut up. Who'd have thought it? Oo—she ayn gonna like that."

11

Next morning, Detective Inspector Rosher stood leaning his bulk against a bulkhead in the Murder Wagon. He had been here all night—not leaning, but lying on the little portable bed which lets down from one wall of a cubicle that doubles as anything you need it for by day: laying out of bodies, grilling people, charging people, incarcerating people; as rest area, camp-gas cooking area, portable darkroom. Many things, and on many types of inquiry; because although commonly called the Murder Wagon, official documentation lists it as Incidents Vehicle. Vehicle, Incidents, to be exact.

It is desirable—nay, it is laid down in the book—that once the wagon is out, a senior rank stays with it at all times. Rosher volunteered, before he was pushed. No joy awaited him in his house on the hill. Dust and a self-cooked fry-up, telly and bed is all. So he stayed, and they brought him supper, and a very good breakfast from the small pub. Now he leaned against the bulkhead. Superintendent Bishop sat in one of the portable chairs that, persevered with, numb the buttocks and leave weals across the backs of the thighs, caused by a bar that runs across the front. In a matching chair sat the Chief Constable. Close beside stood Sergeant Panton, looking alert because it so behooves a man, closeted in close proximity with so much brass.

The Chief was being judicious again. "So we have established a definite connection between the two victims, but so far no clear motive. So far, very little in the way of suspects. Were they both involved in this forgery business?"

"It's well on the cards," said the Archbishop. Scotland Yard had stated categorically that the notes found in the lad Poddy's case came from the same source as what looked like turning into a flood of forged fivers, just beginning to lap at London and Leeds and Bath and Birmingham—all over the place. They were sending a couple of men along.

"Oh, I agree, I agree," the Chief said. "And I have no doubt that if they were, you will soon find out the whys and wherefores. No doubt at all. But—I think we are all agreed—it would be nice if we could clear it before these Scotland Yard wallahs arrive." Very seldom you hear the word wallah nowadays, unless you live in Bournemouth. It is still in daily usage there, among Brigadiers (Ret'd).

"We're doing our best, sir," said the Archbishop, just a trifle stiffly.

"Oh, of course, of course." The Chief had not come here to criticise. He was always very careful not to do that. He came because it made better sense for him to drive out for his morning conference than to disrupt the fieldwork by having everybody come to him. And he spoke because he knew full well that smaller force policemen high and low mislike the assumption of superiority so common in Scotland Yard officers sent to straighten out the turnip-bashers. It is a matter for happy crowing if the case can be cleared and two firm fingers held up as they tramp in through the doorway. "Yes. Mmm. It'll be nice, if we can keep it in the family."

Detective Inspector Rosher was hardly listening. He adhered to his opinion that this daily conference caper was a waste of bloody time. He'd always thought so, and nothing had happened this morning to shake the belief. His mind was ticking over, not fully meshed into gear because there was nothing much to think about, and his eyes wandered idly over the big map pinned to a blackboard mounted on the wall. He cut in abruptly.

"There's no pin in the Wellington place."

"I beg your pardon, Mr. Rosher?" the Chief said, smiling politely. A most mannerly man.

"The farm, sir. The Wellington farm. It doesn't seem to have a pin."

The map was a blown-up portion of the Ordnance Survey sheet for the area; elaborated to show every house in the village, every farm around, every barn, practically every sentry-box privy. There are still a few about, some kept for emergency, some because to remove it would kill Grandad. Old Ossie regularly sat on his. The wood, the lane, were marked with little flags showing where the bodies lay. Every house visited by the house-to-house team bore a white-headed pin. Those called upon a second time by the back-up team (people often remember things, between visits) bore a red-headed pin. Not so numerous, these, the back-up boys were still at it. But the Wellington house had no pin at all.

"Ah," said the Chief. "Perhaps it's fallen out."

Eyes, every one present, automatically cast about the floor beneath the map. Nothing. Not even fluff. "Perhaps," Rosher said, "it hasn't been visited."

All the eyes except Sergeant Panton's turned to Sergeant Panton. His, as he realised why, took on swiftly smothered alarm. The sergeant in the field does not physically organise house-to-house visiting, but he forms the link between upper echelon and the uniform branch who do most of it. Any can for cockup, of course, zooms upward toward the superintendent in overall command; but high brass has the knack of fending it off downward, where it tends to come to rest upon the lowliest vulnerable rank: the sergeant-in-the-field. This sergeant said: "Ah. I think it must have been."

"You *think*?" said Rosher. Plainly, but for the presence of the Old Man he would have added: "You ought to bloody well *know*." The Old Blubbergut bark. But the Chief did not encourage barking.

Superintendent Bishop spoke, mildly. "Is it marked off on the list?"

"I . . . er—" said Sergeant Panton. "The lists are . . . next door. I'll just—"

He moved into action, passing through to the bigger section forming the vehicle's main office. When he returned he was studying the master sheets covering the house-to-house operation. Each pair of officers went out armed with a list. When they came back they reported to a Sergeant Bradym, uniform branch, who yielded up that list, duly ticked. The sergeant in turn ticked this batch of houses off on the master sheets, until ticks proclaimed the whole area covered. "It . . . er . . . doesn't seem to have been listed," he said.

"Ah," said the Chief. A cockup, but a very minor one. No heads would roll. Good leaders accept the fact that all men are fallible. Just don't do it too often.

Superintendent Bishop was another good leader. Percy would have snapped like an iced scorpion. Rosher would have barked. The Archbishop merely carried his mildness forward. "Better do something about it, eh?"

Rosher spoke. "I'll go up."

The superintendent cocked a brow. "Anything special?"

There was no special reason. Not related to the job in hand. But Rosher had never been a man to take put-down easily, as any man who floored him in his boxing days—such men were few— would have testified. It had niggled Rosher, the twins' sending-up, ever since it happened. He fancied a return bout. In his view, too, anybody not automatically exhibiting a proper respect when questioned by any officer, himself in particular, if not overtly bent was probably bent covertly. Come again with basilisk eye, you might not nail them down but you could scare the shit out of 'em. He fancied himself to square matters. "Nothing special," he said. "But if I'm doing back-up, I might as well start there. Save somebody else doing it."

The Chief came to his feet. "Well," he said, "won't keep you gentlemen any longer. I'll get back, the London men will be arriving. You know where I am, if you need me." He placed his hat upon his head, buttoned up his overcoat and they saw him off. As his car drove away, Inspector Rosher said to Sergeant Panton:

"Right, lad. You'd better come with me. Bring your walkie-talkie."

The twins knew last night, as soon as they realised what dog they had shot, that here was trouble. They knew Fiona, they knew how she loved her dog. They were aware of the hysteria that lies beneath the surface in all women, especially virulent in the sexually stressed young girl. They fully expected hysterical reaction. They thought they knew how to handle it.

They had walked up to the Watson-Harvey house this morning after a night shorn of its evening peaceful content. Wary now in their minds, because nobody can really predict what a woman will do, they were nevertheless confident in their combined dominance over her. They had always been able to make her do as they wanted. They'd calm her down.

"I still think perhaps we should have buried it," Timothy said, as they walked up the drive. He had expressed this thought during the night discussion. "Let her think it got lost."

Simon knew that his brother knew why this was impossible. The remark was based entirely upon absurd wishful thinking. Tim was not looking forward to the pending interview, any more than he was. Not that they were emotionally involved; but upset in Fiona could rock their boat. Only a little, because she was sitting in it with them, but rock it nonetheless. He said: "Old Ossie was there."

No need for more. "Maybe we should have buried him, too," said Timothy. And he was not joking. They had wondered, when the burying thought first came up, whether they could vanish Ossie; but at a time like this? And it was no good slipping him money to keep his mouth shut. He couldn't do it. The village would soon know, not only about the dog but about the source of the money he'd be spending in the pub. On top of the previous fiver given, that could stir police interest. A farmer can legally shoot a savaging dog. Why bride an old clown to keep quiet about it?

Fiona was alone in the house. Her mother had gone on a

shopping trip with a friend in the big city who could not be put off—"It will all come right, darling, you'll see. He'll come home, he loves you as much as we do"—and her father was away to his office in the same big city, after a night spent mostly out of doors, seeking the dog.

She found Rover missing when the guests left and she went across to the stable to fetch him. She could see how he got out. Once you knew the upper door swung when you shoved it the thing was obvious. She turned her back on her snorting horse—not a pat did he get that night, no muzzle at a bosom—and raced back to the house.

They would not let her go to look for him. Not safe, they said, for a young girl at this time of night. Daddy will go.

Daddy went. Not to the village, where the policemen were—Rover wouldn't go that way—and not to the Wellingtons', although he reported when he came back that he had been. But he searched all around the area bar these places, and had no luck at all.

Then he had to cover all that ground again, this time in company with Fiona, showing hysteria already—the matter came on top of other stresses—and vowing she would slip out of the window and go, even if she had to smash it, if they locked her in her room.

"There's no question of that, darling," her mother said. "Please, chick, don't get so wrought-up. All right, all right—but only with Daddy. And I'll have some hot cocoa waiting for you when you get back."

Off went Daddy again, given no option. And making no objection, being fond himself of Rover and besotted of his women. It distressed him deeply, the state this one was in. They scoured the entire locality on the near side of the village, taking in the wood where young Poddy was found, crossing the lane into which Tom Nolan floated at a point farther up; and found nothing.

Now, as she was about to leave for further search on her own at the time when the Chief Constable was holding his morning conference, the door chime rang. Her heart leaped up. Perhaps

110

somebody had found him—brought him home. Injured? Not dead—oh—not dead.

Or—perhaps it was the police again. They called last night, but she didn't have to see them. Her father dealt with it, they were asking about Tom Nolan. Gave quite a fillip to the party. It shook her, though.

She hurried to the door, torn between anxieties. Squinted through the little flanking window. There stood Simon and Timothy. She opened the door. "Ah," she said. "I thought it was . . . I thought it might be—"

"Can we come in?" Simon asked. Unusual, for him. Normally, when the door opened they marched straight through.

"Have you seen Rover? He's missing . . . he's . . . we can't find him—"

"It's about Rover," he said.

"Where—where is he? Have you got him? Where—?"

"Let's go through."

The twins moved forward. She stood aside. If pity had been in their makeup it might have surfaced now. She looked sick. Ill, with dark circles under her eyes suddenly too big and unnaturally glittering. All her face had gone thin, it seemed, and the skin was touched with a greenish pallor. She followed them through into the living room; where neither of them sat down. She said: "Have you . . . what about Rover?"

Simon answered. "He was savaging our sheep."

"Sheep?"

"He did it before—the other night. Five Dead. You remember."

"He didn't. He never—"

"We caught him at it. Last night."

"He didn't. You're lying—" She knew what he was saying. Anybody living in a farming community would. The great eyes grew wider yet. "Where is he? What have you done?"

"He . . . got shot."

The wail that came out of her shook even them. "He's dead! He's dead! You killed him!"

Timothy cut in. "We didn't know it was him—it was dark—"

"You've killed him. Killed him!" she screamed. "Oh Christ—he's dead!"

A woman suddenly screaming with pain will rattle the stoutest of men. There's a nerve-shattering, brain-piercing quality to it. And no man really knows how to handle the sudden unbridled emotional convulsion that upends the feminine soul in times of acute distress. Only young men are foolish enough to believe they do.

Simon moved forward, hands reaching. A calming caress—a folding of her in comforting arms—a gentle stroking of her back, moving on unobtrusively to the breasts—while he murmered explanation and regret—to the belly, the thighs—until grief and anger succumbed to her need. She had always been pliant before, they could always set her going. "Fiona, love—" he said. He could coo like a dove, when it suited him. They both could. Timothy stood by, ready to do it as called upon.

They underestimated the situation, hopelessly. Well, they're not alone in that—men have been underestimating the shock-unbalanced woman throughout history. Before the advancing hands reached her she had screamed: "Don't touch me!" and her own hands leaped out to smash him across the face; flailing as he fell back, she shrieking: "You bastards! You bastards!"

Too arrogant to know fear, something like it touched them now. Lightning-fast their minds jumped. Who else was in the house? Nobody, or they would have come running, hearing their pet lamb's high screaming. Simon said with blood coming from his nose: "For Christ's sake—we didn't know. Why'd you let him out?"

"He was a killer," said Timothy.

It was the worst thing to be said. They didn't understand, they simply did not understand. Well, they didn't actually know the whole of it. She had lost more than a loved dog, and this can be grief enough to an only—and so basically lonely—girl-child. She had lost a lover, her one true lover. She went on screaming. "Get out! Bastards! Get out!"

112

That telepathy, most acute in times of alarm, flashed between the brothers. Get away now, before somebody came. Handkerchief to his nose, Simon said: "Come on, Tim." They moved to the door. He turned to address Fiona, an undertone of harsh warning in his voice. "Don't do anything silly, Fifi. Mind what you say. We'll see you later." They called her Fifi, sometimes. Quite a few people did, notably a college lover who plied her with black underwear, rosette garters and high-heeled shoes with pom-poms on.

"Get out! Get out!" she screamed, seeming about to reach for vases. They left, and when they were gone she collapsed into agonised weeping.

When Inspector Rosher and Sergeant Panton arrived in the Wellingtons' yard, Old Ossie was plying a stiff broom, clearing away the mess of mud and dead leaves left by the storm. He called across: "If you want Mr. Simon and Mr. Timothy, they gorn out."

"Ah," said the inspector. "Where'd they go?"

"Dunno, they doan tell me. They was gorn when I got here. Up to Miss Fiona's, likely. Shot her dog last night, he were arter them ole sheep. Got him in here." The battered cloth cap inclined, indicating the barn. "Reckon they'll want to know what she wants done with him. Mind you, he ayn good for much no more."

Shot her dog, eh? Well, that was legal, they couldn't be lifted for that. "Is Mrs. Wellington in?"

"Never go out, do she? Can't *get* out, most of the time. Hee hee hee." And the old rip turned again to his sweeping.

The two policemen approached the door. Inspector Rosher advanced his thick and hairy finger to jab the bell push. They stood in a weak gleam of sunshine wan with belated acceptance of encroaching winter until Mrs. Wellington appeared to blink into painful daylight, when Rosher snatched off the black hat and said with hardly a trace of his telephone manner—ladies who proved themselves unworthy no longer qualified for it: "Mrs. Wellington. Good morning."

"They're out," she said. "My boys are out."

"Doesn't matter, it's only a routine call. We'll step in for a minute, if we may."

Even bulky policemen insinuate themselves through doors very cleverly, when they want to. Two big bodies were in the glum hall before she had time to protest, if that is what she meant to do. She blinked at them again—with a brain permanently fogged, probably she did not see how they got there—and repeated: "They're out. My boys—they're out."

"We'll go through, shall we?"

Trained by her sons and their father before them in obedience to masculine command, she balanced herself before letting go of the door, measuring the journey between here and the living room with a weak and watery eye. Poor old duck, thought Sergeant Panton: what a state to get into. Better off dead.

"Well now madam," said Inspector Rosher in the living room, "we are here to see whether you can help us in our inquiries. Do you recognise this man?" He slipped one of the photographs out of its envelope and handed it to her.

She blinked at it, trying for focus. "Who is it?" she asked.

Well—that, in a way, was the problem. The Poddys had furnished the name, but that was all. Even the hospital knew him only as a vagrant, there seemed to be no background details. No personal connections, even, apart from his friendship with a fellow murder victim; and if Teddy Poddy knew all about him, and he about Teddy Poddy, neither was in condition to pass information. "His name is Thomas Nolan. He was found dead yesterday, as no doubt you know."

Still striving to focus on the picture, she said: "They don't tell me anything. They're out. He looks very young to be dead."

"Sit down, madam, sit down." Because she was wobbly on her feet. If she never went out, unless he came here she wouldn't know this Nolan. Even if she'd met him—and she wouldn't have—any kind of memory of it would be a confused blur. It's possible, the inspector thought, that she doesn't even remember me.

She dispelled the notion. "You're the policeman. That's what you are, you're the one that looks like a monkey." She made it to her chair and sat down.

Sergeant Panton swallowed a snort. Rosher skewered him with that hard eye. He said, with some asperity: "That is as may be, madam. Your sons are out, you say. Do you know where?" No sense would come out of her.

"Business," she said. She was shaking a tiny dome shaped like a flying saucer from a small envelope. "Making money. Money. They like to make money."

Probe while you can. "Do they have other business interests? Other than sheep?"

She was displaying the little capsule. "I've got three of these, today," she said, "because I've got a headache. They give them to me. My boys. For my headaches. They look after their mother. They're good boys."

That's no aspirin, Sergeant Panton was thinking. It might be one of those telly cure-alls, but I know bloody well it's not. Inspector Rosher was glimmering his big brown teeth, gone jovial. "I've got a bit of a headache myself. Can I have one?"

She sat up straight and answered with a fine dignity. "Certainly not. They're for *my* headache."

He could easily have taken one; but careful, careful with that sort of thing. For all he knew, some goggle-eyed social worker might visit her. He didn't know, but it seemed quite likely. He'd never been ruled by the book, but when it came to strident allegation by a do-gooder that he robbed a frail old lady—old before her time, but old certainly and frail definitely—of her very medicants while she was in a relapsed condition: to wit, pissed: this he did not need. And once already, to his great cost, a sergeant had been marched in to bear witness against him. So he said: "Well—mind how you wash it down. I won't take up any more of your time. Good morning."

That terrible travesty of the gracious hostess gushed from her again. "Goodbye, Mr. . . . er— Do come again." All toothy beaming and dizzy eyes.

There really was no point in staying, with work to be done.

The lads could be visited later, if necessary. Rosher let himself out, wondering as he crossed the hall whether he should not grab the opportunity for a swift shufti around the house. Sons who feed their mother bombers to be consumed with alcohol are worth thinking about, they might have all sorts of little bits tucked away. But it takes time to uncover little bits, even if they are there; and the buggers might well come in when he was rooting in the bed-rooms. Trespass. Or the old girl (much younger than Rosher, but he thought of her as the old girl) might not be so immobilised as she looked, you never can tell with drunks. And besides: he was not too sure of Sergeant Panton, tramping through the hall at his side. So he went through the hall and out, leaving the sergeant to close the door behind them.

Old Ossie was gone now. Hurriedly and happily. Wondering if the coppers were calling just for routine, as they called on him last night, or whether they were going to pinch the twins, or what. He had shoved a wedge of leaves onto his shovel—it happened even as the policemen entered the house—and lifted it, to be trans-ferred to the wheelbarrow. He would not have seen the crumpled-up paper had it not been stuck to the back of the shovel, uppermost when he turned it over. But he did see it; and because such a scrap turned out, long ago, to be a pound note, he never threw the like away without scrutiny.

Today was better—better—five times better than a pound note, even though in the dear dead days a pound bought so much more.

Now indeed the cup of Old Ossie gushed over. Fate was beaming upon him as never before in all the long years since his father, being told he was on the way, beat his brow in despair, crying: "You daft bitch—another bloody mouth to feed." There were murders brightening the days, dead dogs and sudden fivers. Oh, hee hee hee.

He could apply that broom with astonishing force and vigour, when he wanted to. This new wealth inserted carefully into his decrepit wallet was muddy, and very wet. But he could clean it, he could dry it out. Hee hee hee hee hee. By the time the policemen

116

came out of the house the yard was swept, the broom was stashed, the barrow was stowed, and he was gone.

Inspector Rosher said to Sergeant Panton when he had resettled the black hat and they were tramping down the drive: "What did you think of the aspirin?"

"In my opinion—" the sergeant began.

"I don't want your opinion," said Inspector Rosher. "I just want to know what you think of it."

"Sonoril. Diconol. Tunil. Something like that."

"Hrrmph," said Inspector Rosher. He often did, when disconcerted. He'd thought the young man had not noticed, he had meant to demonstrate the superior powers of observation that fitted a man for superior rank. And the bugger named names he didn't even know himself. Now Panton was adding to it.

"Very dodgy, mixing them with alcohol."

"I am well aware of that," said Inspector Rosher. "I am very well aware of that. Get your walkie-talkie out, I want to know if she gets 'em on prescription." If not, he'd be on those two young buggers' backs. Not half.

Sergeant Panton produced his personal radio, thinking: Why didn't we just ask her? But I suppose it wouldn't have done much good, the state she was in.

If the twins had gone straight home from Fiona's house they must have found Inspector Rosher again in the living room, having a word with their mother. Whether or not this would have alarmed them in their shaken state is a moot point, and one not worth arguing because they had no inkling that he was there. Shaken, they made a long trek home through woods and over the hills. What they were really doing was taking a bromide, using physical exercise to restore mental equilibrium.

They talked as they went, rather more than usually was necessary between them. Shocked people often become loquacious. And they were realising that they now had things to worry about.

They were playing the sort of game where right hand does not know there is such a thing as left hand. The only person who

117

might have stumbled upon both in action was Mother, and they had taken care of that problem.

She always loved her little tipple; but they fastened her tight to the bottle, supplemented as they felt necessary, after Fiona introduced them to the drugs caper. It wasn't difficult, she was so pleased when they approved her having just another teeny-weeny one. Even brought her one, smiling as she yearned for them to smile upon her—the smiling had stopped, of late—when she demurred without conviction, or looked like tapping the heels.

Timothy said, coming down through the woods: "She's bloody mad. She's as nutty as Teddy was. And Tom Nolan. Suppose she starts talking—"

"She won't," his brother said. "She's as deep in as we are."

She was not, actually; but certainly she was in very deep. It was she who gave them the drugs connection. A lot of smoking and a little jabbing went on at her college, materials supplied by a nice man who appeared from time to time in a handy cafe. She mentioned this; they brooded, requested an introduction, pointing out to her the potential. To encapsulate—a lot of checking and cross-checking went on before the source people agreed to use them, and they had to lay out all they could muster. These things are not done just like that. It suited the man to make one bulk delivery now and again at a rendezvous, to have somebody else take off his hands the risk and labour of distribution by personal contact. He had form for drug offenses—they had no form of any sort. So they were in business, doing very well. Branched out, when the opportunity arose, into the funny money lurk. Didn't mention it to the drugs man. Not likely.

About the funny money, Fiona knew nothing; and because of this, and because she had drawn personally none of her own arranged third share of the drugs money (she could not suddenly begin to whop large sums into her little bank account, or stash a cache in the house. Doting parents are into everything except sex), they were much deeper in than she was. As a matter of truth—the ease with which they manipulated her in this as well as in sex contributed to their belief that they could handle her this morning.

118

The money they were supposed to be stowing for her reposed in various accounts of their own, in far-flung places under various names, and they had no intention of disgorging. What could she do, if she found out? Tell the police? She had too much to lose. Simon just said so.

"Yes, but if she's done her nut—look at bloody Nolan." His brother making no answer, Timothy brooded awhile before voicing the thought he knew was in the matching mind as surely as it was in his own. "Perhaps we ought to—"

That Simon snapped his reply was evidence of the upset in him. They did not snap at each other, these two. "Don't be a twat. Bloody coppers everywhere? Don't be a twat."

Not long after the twins left, while they were still tramping the stripped-out woods and suddenly soggy moors and fields, the stress of panic added itself to Fiona's grief. Fear had been chilly in her ever since the police called last night. They had come, she was certain until her father reported after dealing with them, to take her in. Now they came again.

She was weeping still, her mother not yet home, when she raised streaming eyes to the living room window and saw through rainbows the two solid men in uniform coming up the drive. In a blind terror she rushed up the stairs and locked herself into the bathroom. Daft thing to do, did she think they were going to smash the front door down? It was only the back-up team. All they did was ring the bell, and after a time they went away.

When Inspector Rosher and Sergeant Panton got back to the Murder Wagon they found the usual clutch of rubbernecks standing at a distance, kept there by two guardian constables, and undisciplined children belonging to them sky-larking nearer, some for a dare dashing right up to jump in the air, trying to see in through the windows before capering away again. One of the policemen was Constable Phillis, the local man. Rosher said in passing: "Clear these kids out of it."

"That's all right," said Constable Phillis, "but it's not so

119

bloody easy." And he was right. You can't clump kids any longer, and rubberneck parents are just the type to howl in the tit-papers if you do. That can cost you. Nor can you chase them. They are very nimble, they can make you look a berk, all the audience tittering. Stripped of dignity, what becomes of authority?

"Warn the parents," Rosher snapped.

Constable Phillis was on his home patch. So never mind that this was Rosher, the legendary Old Blubbergut who fell, and rose again from the dead, and was seen black-hatted on telly and in all the papers. Nobody snapped with impunity at him, on his own patch. "You sort 'em out for me, I will," he said, stiffly. They were not village kids, the little bastards.

"Hrrrmph," said Rosher, and passed on. He found Chief Superintendent Bishop within, sitting at the portable desk among the ever-increasing bumph that accumulates horribly round any major case and frowning over his thinking. He held a sheet of paper and his eyes were on it, but his mind more than likely was gone far beyond. He said:

"Ah. How's it going?"

"Well enough," said Rosher. Sergeant Panton said nothing. His not to make reply. "Covered the Wellingtons, thought we'd call in to see what gives." He had further back-up calls to make, but a cup of tea would be nice, before he carried on. Back-up for him was only killing time, keeping the mind flexed and the body from relaxing. He knew it, Archie Bishop knew it. The super said:

"Your call. The Wellington lady. She doesn't seem to be registered with the local doctor."

She would not have to be registered with any doctor, if she spurned the joys lavished by the National Health Service. "Is she a private patient?"

"Not with him, he's never seen her. Or the sons. We're working on it, they may be registered in the town or somewhere. What's it about?"

Rosher told him. "She's an alcoholic. Had a very funny aspirin. I couldn't get hold of one, but it looked to me like Sonoril or something. Of that nature. She says the boys give 'em to her."

120

"Do they indeed? With alcohol?"

"Uh-huh."

"Interesting. Well worth a thought or two." The Archbishop's tone implied approval; so Rosher did not bridle when he added: "But that's not really our business, just at the moment. We seem to be a trifle bogged. Nothing much in all the bumph—nothing from anywhere. Nothing from your bank idea, this far—" Notice again the tact, the giving of credit where due, the holding back from suggesting that the idea had proved useless—"still no obvious motive. Or motives. Still no details on the second victim. I'm going over to the hospital, to interview some of the people who knew them both."

Rosher actually glimmered a tooth. "That'll be pleasant."

"Mm." The super worked his own smile. Better practised than Rosher's, it came more easily. "Thought of giving it to you, but why should you have all the treats? The quack there doesn't seem to know much about either of 'em, but somebody might. Suggest you get yourselves a cupper, there's some in the galley. Or there was, but you can't trust anybody these days. I'll get away when I've looked this lot over, leave you to mind the shop."

"Right," said the Inspector, and he preceded Sergeant Panton into that little cubical which now was a camping-gas galley, where the tea in the metal pot had brewed to a brooding black, just the way he liked it.

Fruitless, the super's visit to the hospital. Just as fruitless, Rosher's further follow-up visits. A day of dull, routine frustration. In town, the two Scotland Yard men arrived at the station, lunched in the canteen where both left the chef's Special Apple Crumble almost untouched (it is an acquired taste—very few acquire it), had a few more words with the Chief Constable and went home, bearing sample notes.

But nothing at all happened in Hutton Fellows. Until, of course, the evening, when things began to bubble up quite suddenly. That's the way it is, with police work.

12

It was fully two hours after the back-up team sent Fiona scurrying to lock herself into the lavatory when Mrs. Watson-Harvey came home. The girl had unlocked and emerged by then, of course, but her mental condition was not improved. If anything, it had worsened through the hours spent on her own. After a time of listening to her weeping and railing against the twins and weeping again, of trying without success to soothe her, of proferred aspirin knocked out of the hands and cooling draughts dashed aside, her mother rang Daddy at his office. He drove home at once; and after a little more time, worried, they sent for the doctor.

There is only one doctor in Hutton Fellows: a young one, with a beard. A devout Christian, settled in a country practise because of his health. Which he should have known about, if anybody did. A man of high principles who needed mothering and got it from an older wife. The Watson-Harveys' regular doctor lived in the town and was altogether more rugged; but at this time of the year he tended to vanish, shooting on the moors. That is where he was today; so they rang this Doctor Harnet.

The young doctor arrived, and did a sensible thing. His patient was not being helped by the hovering of her parents. The mother, indeed, was herself in a highly emotional condition, and the father not much better. Daughter, mother, father reacting upon each other were stewing up an ambience of rising hysteria, so he asked the parents to wait downstairs before seating himself by

Fiona's bed—her mother had put her to bed—and averting his gaze from her glorious, heaving bosom while he let her sob her heart out. Doctors are only human, and his wife, whose bra was twin egg-cups, shared with him a truly spiritual relationship. Besides, there was his health.

When he had administered a sedative he went downstairs and gave a tablet or two to Mrs. Watson-Harvey. Mr. Watson-Harvey had armoured himself with a stiff whisky, and so did not need any. He was pouring another, right now. The doctor made reassuring noises while he scribbled an illegible prescription, declined a tot and was let out. He went home with great disturbance in his mind. Mr. Watson-Harvey rushed off at once to the town, where Harbottle, Chemist, filled the prescription. God knows how they do it. But perhaps it does not matter, so long as the medicine looks right.

Another nice house, the one where the doctor lives. A little Queen Anne gem, wisteria all over the front and a garden at the back where grow many herbs, tended one afternoon a week by Old Ossie—currently at home in his frowsy cottage, drying his fiver—and for the rest of the time by the older wife, who met him at the door with her hair still damp from a fresh application of Delia Fanshawe's Special Preparation. Keeps the Grey Away. It also adds lustre. She cannot relax, the woman with a young and (some said) handsome husband. She said brightly:

"Hallo, darling. Everything all right?"

"Yes, dear," he said; but something was bothering him, she knew it.

Well, it would all come out in the end. He would bring it to her, as he brought all his troubles. She would not press him, it only made him irritable. "Go on into your study, dear," she said. "I'll bring you a cup of Bovril."

It was not until they sat at high tea that he unburdened. She always gave him high tea, so that he did not have to tackle evening surgery without something solid in his stomach. Not that surgery was all that arduous, they are a healthy lot in Hutton Fellows. Generally speaking.

"I think, really, that you should tell the police, dear," she

123

said. "That funny one who was on the television, he's in the village, I saw him."

"My oath, dear," he said, not using an archaic epithet, but referring to the oath taken. "What I hear from a patient is strictly private." He manifestly was upset, doing no more than toy with her Welsh Rarebit.

"But in a case like this . . . if you believe it's a serious matter—"

"It could be life and death," he said. "On the other hand, I have only her word to go on. And she is temporarily unbalanced by the killing of her dog."

"Perhaps you should ring the vicar."

"No, no, no." The irritability was showing already. Truth to tell, he did not like her very much. And he hadn't much time for the vicar. "It's nothing to do with the vicar. And the police wouldn't be too impressed—an hysterical girl's unsupported word."

"They would interview her, dear, wouldn't they? They'd get to the bottom of it."

"That's just the trouble. In my view, the child is a latent hysteric in a state of shock." Young doctors, given an admiring audience, can be enormously pompous. "Being faced suddenly with the stress of police interviewing can do her no good. My first responsibility is to my patient. What becomes of trust?"

"What about the other party?"

"I know, I know. I am well aware of the other party."

By early evening, the rain was back. Drizzle this time, falling through brown mist which looked like thickening into the first of the late-autumn fogs that hang so drearily in these valleys. Chief Superintendent Bishop had returned from his visit to the big city, with copious notes unobtrusively gathered for him by an impassive policeman who knew well how to blend with the furniture while he scribbled shorthand. These notes must all be transcribed now, to enable the super to study them.

A waste of time. But possibly not, since several people still in the hospital had gossiped freely—eagerly, even, welcoming a break in the sad monotony of their days—about the lads' friendship.

For this kind of work, a police station offers rather better facilities than does a Murder Wagon. A man concentrates better in his own quiet office with his own big desk to spread things on, knowing exactly where the ashtray is, than in a small corner amid booted comings and goings in and out of a confined space. The transcribing policeman can spread a little, too. And should anything break, it will probably be known first at the station anyway. No time will be lost.

So the superintendent went off to the town, taking the short-hand man with him. Inspector Rosher would be here through the night again; so when Old Ossie set out to spend his fortuitous fiver, the inspector was once more as he liked to be: in sole charge. And things began to bubble.

Old Ossie arrived at the smaller pub not long after opening time. He had made a good job of his fiver, washing it very carefully in his scullery where the flood water had seeped away by now through the floor, scraping and rubbing the lingering marks, even ironing it to restore some kind of crackle. By the time he was finished, it looked almost as new.

There was nobody else in the bar when he entered. In this day of inflated prices, even pubs where the beer is cosseted and dearly loved do no business until well into the licensed hours, on wet and chilly evenings. The fire was lit, the curtains were drawn, fresh sawdust was down in the public bar and the landlord set in position, standing behind his mellow counter with the first testing-pint (he tested frequently all through the day, to guard against sudden deterioration) half consumed. It could have been a film set, somebody having forgotten to book the extras.

Old Ossie walked into it with his crusty old cap and the sack worn over his shoulders bedewed with the sullen drizzle. He did not see how nicely the lamplight played on shadowed beams, on old oak settles and twinkling glasses and the bottles set behind the bar, but he saw the landlord and said: "–'Evening, George."

The landlord lowered the glass from his lips. "You're early," he said.

"Open, ain't you?" said Old Ossie. "Bin working, getting me regulars straight. Give us a whisky."

A whisky? A pint, was Ossie's order. Bitter. Never varied. "How long you been drinking whisky?"

"Never you mind about that. You just give me a whisky. Double. And a pint."

"Ain't pension day, is it? You better count your money, whisky don't come cheap."

"I got the money. Bin working, ayn I?" Indignant, Old Ossie produced the laundered note and slapped it down on the bar. "That's a fiver, that is."

"Well, well, well. Well, well. Mind how you go with it, then. Don't get pissed in here, I won't have you getting pissed in here."

"I'll get pissed where I like," the old man snapped. "It's a free country."

The landlord turned away, to measure out the whisky. He drew the pint. He picked up the note. "Good health," he said. "Stick to beer is my advice, spirits'll wreck it."

Old Ossie was rich, and the rich can afford arrogance. "When I wants your advice," he said, "I'll arst for it." He swigged off a little bitter, making room; tipped the whisky into the pint glass. A practise that makes Scotsmen rend their sporrans, but one common among the more affluent countrymen in this part of the world.

Not only Scotsmen object to the habit. Dedicated ale-men detest it. "You ain't doing that beer no good," the landlord said. "If I'd known you was going to do that to it you could have done it up the road. Cat's piss they serve, it don't matter." He was studying the fiver. Had it come from any other customer it would have gone straight into the drawer, but two fivers from Ossie in the space of two non-pension days: this was something rare and strange. He'd been working, yes. Presumably somebody paid it to him. Even so— His eyes suddenly gimletted into focus, like little bloodshot

126

camera lenses going for the smallest stop. "Hang on a minute—hang on—don't drink no more. This is a bleeding fiddle."

Old Ossie reared up immediately. Underlying the arrogance of the nouveau riche is always an insecurity, based upon the fear that their sins will be found out and all that lovely money snatched away. The poorer they have been, the greater the fear and the need for bluster; and Old Ossie had been very poor, all his life. No unions, when he ploughed and scattered. "Fiddle?" he bristled. "What bleeding fiddle? You wanna watch your bleeding lip." He raised his glass hurriedly. If it was going to be snatched away, the buggers weren't going to get it all.

"Put it down, put it down," the landlord cried. He reached out his hands in supplication; but Ossie moved to show his back, lowering the fluid level rapidly. The landlord lifted his voice. "MABEL!"

His wife appeared, at the door back of the bar. "What's up, what's up?" she said.

"Get on to the police," cried the man who stood beside her at the altar, when he had hair and a nose like Robert Taylor and she wore Small Women's with all her own teeth. "The old bugger's done me for a double with a duff fiver."

"More fool you," she said. But she fixed Old Ossie with a hard eye.

"I ain't, I ain't," Ossie said. The liquor was low in the glass by now. "Give it here—there'm nothing wrong with ut. A gentleman give it me. I can pay." He drew from his pocket some of his own earned store.

The landlord took it; handed over the note; moved to the till and brought a little change. "You've tried it on before," he said, "haven't you? Better burn that thing, when you get it home."

There was the root cause of his quick reaction. Another customer passing him the note would have been told, if it had been spotted at all, quite pleasantly that it was bad. The matter rectified, interesting conversation would have ensued, the customer trying to sort out what bugger laid it upon him. But Old Ossie had indeed tried to work a little flanker before, sidling off without paying and the like. Now he darted tortoise eyes sideways as he pulled off what was left in the glass.

"Ought to be handed in, by rights," the wife said.

The alarm bells jangled in Ossie's old mind. They were going to take it away from him, his wealth with which there was nothing wrong and if there was he'd find a way to spend it. There'd be questions—the police—they'd make him say he found it and drop him straight in. He gulped the last of his drink, said: "Nothing wrong with it . . . it was give me . . . I bin working."

"If somebody give you that one," the landlord told him, "you better go and sort him out. Who was it?"

"Mind your own business." Old Ossie turned and headed for the door, pausing before he went through it to say: "You won't see me in here no more." With which diabolical threat, he vanished into the murk. Nobody rushed after him, to plead on bended knees.

"Silly old sod," the landlord said as he drew himself another test.

"You shouldn't have told him to burn it," said his wife.

"He's harmless enough."

"*He* is. What about the fiver? You can drop in it if they find out you handled a duff fiver and handed it back without saying nothing. *And* told him to burn it. That's a criminal offense." She did not know if it was, and she didn't know if it was not; but a woman in the long embattlement of marriage develops a stunning ability to concoct a throwing brick from the veriest wisp of straw.

"Bloody rubbish," said her husband; but he felt a stir of unease. He was very tender about his license, which is why he was so firm about time, gentlemen, please. His record had no spot, and he meant to keep it that way. Should he ever lose his license, how could he conduct his tests? "Still," he added, "I suppose it can't do no harm, to give Ted Phillis a ring." It never does harm, to smirk toward the police.

"Why don't you ring the one who was on the telly? He was in here. He's in that thing they've got on the green."

128

But a publican known the value of cultivating the local man. Don't jump over his back for the sake of an incomer gone tomorrow, just because of the telly. You have to live with the local man until your liver gives out, or he drops dead chasing a poacher up a very steep hill.

There had been little activity in the Murder Wagon, since Chief Superintendent Archie Bishop left Detective Inspector Rosher in charge. The back-up teams finished long ago; their reports were typed in quadruplicate, copy to the Archbishop, copy to Rosher, copy to the Chief Constable and one for the files. More bumph. Bumph, bumph, bumph, and rarely anything in it. But woe to you if something is, and you missed it. And you throw nothing away.

Per example: bumph from long ago and far afield was yielding its harvest of yet more bumph even now. In Birmingham, in Harrogate and in Exeter the police had matched up Tom Nolan's circulated fingerprints. In Birmingham, five years ago when he was sixteen, he punched some poor bird badly in pursuit of his oats and was done for it. In Harrogate two years back he was rolled up for pot smoking. He was done again in Exeter a year ago, after beating up a bank manager with whom he was sharing home, hearth and bed. Helped himself to the bank manager's wallet, picked up the silver and left. They nicked him on tip-off from a pawn shop, high again but on harder drugs. Count in the offense that sent him to hospital by nod of a kindly judge, he had quite a record.

All this came to Superintendent Bishop in the station, and thence to Rosher by phone, at intervals during the early evening. They discussed it, and agreed that for their purpose it might mean a lot, or it might mean nothing. Nolan, it seemed, was a nasty young man and on drugs. Teddy Poddy, his friend, had drugs in him when he died. Connection? Were they concerned together in a little caper, did they get themselves done by crossing backers? Some do—drugs syndicates can be very vicious.

Maybe. But plenty of youngsters are on drugs nowadays,

quite independently. No real evidence that after the hospital friendship they were ever in touch, in spite of Tom Nolan's having been seen in the village. Few hospital friendships survive, people often hate to recall the circumstances under which they existed.

Well: social workers, prison officers, probation officers and all the official bumph-makers called upon to deal with recalcitrants were being seen or still to be seen in Birmingham, in Harrogate, in Exeter. They might come up with something. Meantime, said Superintendent Bishop to Inspector Rosher, it gives us something else to think about. I've got the drugs squad on it, he said.

"Could they have been working a blackmail lurk?" Rosher wondered. He was thinking of Teddy's note.

"Possible, possible," the Archbishop said. "Anything's possible. I'm going home now. You know where to get me if you need me." No senior officer can ever leave a junior without pointing this out.

There the matter rested, Rosher sitting in his little cubicle mulling it all over with the telephone close handy, when Constable Ted Phillis arrived with Old Ossie in tow.

He was no fool, Constable Phillis. Twenty years a policeman on a rural patch does not necessarily turn a man into a turnip. No dream of high rank in this one, no desire for it. He had his Mini-van, his garden, a minimum of supervision. It was enough. But he was not averse to kudos, if they were offered; especially kudos in a case much, much bigger than normally came his way. Certainly, he did not relish handing them over to a bloody great gorilla who bared his teeth at him in his own backyard.

So he did not ring Rosher after the call from the landlord. He put the phone down in his little police house and reached for his tunic. His wife said: "Where are you going?"

"Over to Hutton Fellows," he told her. "Something's come up."

"What about your supper?"

"Stick it in the oven," he said. "Keep it hot. If I'm not back before the gravy dries up turn the gas out." He kissed her, and she was still worth kissing being not too plump and more comely than the run of policemen's wives, and drove through the rain to Hutton Fellows, arriving at Old Ossie's picturesque but frowsy cottage just as Rosher picked up the phone, for his talk with the doctor's wife. A few minutes later he left again, urging Old Ossie along.

Having no number for the Murder Wagon, she had rung the station asking to be put through to whoever was in charge of the big vehicle on the green. Superintendent Bishop was on his way home and incommunicado until he got there. Inspector Young Alec Cruse was still about, controller of the HQ team and waiting to see if anything else came in relating to Thomas Nolan, 21. He, scrupulously ethical in his dealings with the man, said: "Put her through to Mr. Rosher." Probably some kind of crank call, but Rosher for the nonce was commander in the field. Ergo: she belonged to him.

She said: "Who is speaking, please?"

Rosher had merely said hallo. He elaborated. "Detective Inspector Rosher."

"Are you the one," she fluted, "who appeared on television, in a black hat?"

"I have been on television, madam." The world is full of mutters.

But this was no mutter. This was an aging woman with an outsize in maternal instincts, fastened hungrily in childlessness upon a young and rather fragile husband who was suffering a crisis of conscience, he being Christian in the humourless way that almost commands such crises. He was out at present, rehearsing Handel with the choir; and she, worrying about him as was her wont, had come to the conclusion that *she* was bound by no oath, and she'd better do something if he was to sleep tonight. Other wives have other ways of knocking their husbands out, but how many men are so lucky? She spoke into the inspector's hairy ear.

"Ah. Good. I was hoping it would be. I am Mrs. Harnet."

"Mrs.—?"

"Harnet. Doctor Harnet's wife. My husband attended a girl in

131

the village today, one of the better houses. A Miss Watson-Harvey. She was undergoing a fit of hysteria. I believe her dog had been shot."

"Uh-huh." Hairnet? Hairnet? Harnet—local G.P.

"What?"

"What what?"

"I didn't catch what you said."

"I said yes. We know about the dog."

"Ah. Mm. Well, apparently she was seriously disturbed. So were her parents, he had to get rid of them. When they were gone she was letting off—"

"Letting off?"

"Fulminating. Against two local twins, I expect you know them. The Wellington boys. They are the ones who shot her dog. I expect you know that. But she was quite beyond reason, calling them killers. Murderers. He—my husband—pointed out that the death of a dog is, of course, entirely reprehensible, but not classified as murder. He was trying to calm her, you see, before administering a sedative, he has a wonderful bedside manner, very soothing. But she said he didn't know what she knew, and they were monsters, and they were deliberately killing their mother by encouraging her to drink—well, she does drink, of course, everyone knows that—but they give her drugs with it. To keep her from knowing what they are up to. Hallo? Are you stiff there?"

"I am still here, madam," said Rosher.

"Ah. Good. I thought you'd been cut off."

"Did she say what they are up to?"

"No. She shied away after that, he said. Told him to go away, that she wanted to be alone, you know how they are. Well, perhaps you don't. But she said another thing that worries him. After she said they were murderers she said ask Tom Nolan. And then—he says—she seemed to retreat because she knew she was saying too much. He had that feeling."

"Why did your husband not report all this to us, madam?" Rosher had his pomposity working now. It came to the fore as always when he turned stiff with a member of the public.

132

"The girl is his patient. He felt that a sudden visit from you, or whatever you do, would worsen her condition.

"And what about the condition of the other lady?"

"That's just what I said, it's worrying him terrible. That's why I took it upon myself to clear the matter up. I won't have him worried, his sleep is important."

"It is surely more important, madam, to report anything of this nature—"

"Yes. Well—that's all right, then, isn't it? I've done it." And she put the phone down.

Rosher, not expecting it, thought she had fallen victim to a pulled-out plug; but he had no time to go further than that. Almost before he realised that she was gone, Constable Phillis came in with Old Ossie, saying: "Reckon you'd better have a look at this, Mr. Rosher."

He passed the note. Inspector Rosher took it with one hand, the other still holding the phone to his ear. When he saw what it was the instrument went back into its cradle, forgotten. "Where'd you get this?" he demanded.

"Old Ossie here. Tried to pass it in the pub."

"Nothing wrong with it," Old Ossie quavered. Scared now. "It was give me. I bin working."

When Old Blubbergut barked with his little eyes glittering, men much tougher than Ossie quivered. Not little old men, either. Men at the very height of their naughty powers. "Who gave it to you?"

Frightened as he was, the old man advanced his little evasion. He didn't know how it had all gone wrong, but the blood of his father and his father's father's father scurried about in him, saying don't tell the bastards nothing. "Nobody," he said. "I ayn done nothing."

Constable Phillis was thinking: you don't have to lean on the poor old sod, you nasty bastard. Wish I'd had it out of him now, before I brought him in. He spoke, almost on a note of protest. This was one of his people. "Come on, Ossie, spit it out. You'll only get yourself in trouble." And to Rosher: "Says a gentleman give it to him."

The bark came again, redirected. "I'll handle this, Constable." So like a gorilla, the face turned back to Ossie. "Know what the penalty is for passing forgeries? Seven years. If you're lucky. Now: who gave it to you?"

Old Ossie visibly shrank. So heavy a hammer, for such a little nut. Well, he brought it on himself. After all, he owed no particular loyalty to the Wellingtons. Evasion was purely blood-reaction. "Mr. Simon give it me," he quavered. "Him and Mr. Timothy." Still the evasion, you see. He couldn't simply say he found it in the Wellingtons' yard; which is a very different thing from their giving it. He knew well enough that trouble can come from pocketing picked-up money, regardless of whether it be good or bad. So he evaded all over again.

It was enough for Rosher, coming right on top of that phone call and at a time when he had the field to himself. He asked no more questions. One new bark, and no doubt he could have had the truth out of Ossie, but the twins were blotted in his book, and when somebody blotted he was always very willing to believe whatever gave him excuse to more than square the matter. They were doping their lush old mother—Tom Nolan was mentioned. And they handed out funny money. He did not care that they would be mad to do it here, now, in their own village. It was enough.

And nobody was sitting on his back. He'd be up there and doing it his way before Archie Bishop could drive out from town.

He spoke to Constable Phillis as he got up from the portable desk. "Keep him in here until I get back."

"Er—yeah. Right."

The inspector shrugged into his battleship-grey raincoat. Picked up his black hat and stepped out into the main body of the vehicle, where the night man sat on duty at the switchboard eating a small pork pie. Close by, Sergeant Panton worked on a crossword puzzle. He looked up when the apelike figure suddenly appeared. Rosher snapped: "Put that down, I want you with me."

And to the operator: "Raise Superintendent Bishop. You've got his number on your pad."

The operator swallowed the last of his pie as he dialled. When the super's wife came to the phone to say he's here, just hold on a moment, he stuffed in another of his little plugs and indicated the extension from which the Archbishop would speak. Rosher picked it up; said after a moment:

"Ah. Mr. Bishop. A little matter's come up, I'm on my way to deal with it."

The Archbishop had been home only long enough to slip off his jacket, don his dressing gown, accept his wife's offer of a cup of tea and settle in front of the telly. He said: "What sort of thing?"

"I think it might be worthwhile if I have a few words with the Wellington twins. One of the villagers tried to pass a funny fiver, says he got it from them."

"Does he, by jove? I'll come over."

"No hurry. I'll bring them down to here, if there's anything in it." No snap at all in the inspector's voice. The way to minimise a happening is to speak about it calmly, as mere routine, bringing no need for anybody to sweat. And to leave out details. Use as off-hand a voice as you can. Rosher, in pursuit of kudos, perfected the technique long ago.

Archie Bishop was a Chief Superintendent, and no man rises so far who is not pretty cute. He said: "Does it tie in with the killings?" After all, murder is why the wagon was there, murder is what they were working on. Rosher was a solid man, within his limitations; but the matter of forgery was a by-issue, belonging to Scotland Yard by now.

"Possibly, sir. Possibly. Poddy was their cousin." Shtum, about the Watson-Harvey girl's mention of Tom Nolan. Speaking of that could have the Archbishop leaping about with his skates on.

"All right," said the superintendent. "If you need me, then ring again and I'll come out. Otherwise, you might as well send them in to the station. Always supposing you have reason. I'll be there." Fair enough—the wagon was engaged, and cramped already. And the station was where the lads would wind up, if anywhere. Why complicate, with roads all covered in mud?

"Will do," Rosher said, and hung up. Better than he'd hoped—the old bugger wasn't coming out at all. The can was lifted away from the shoulder, all was square with the book. Here we go, then. "You know where I am, lad, if you need me. Look up the number now, they'll have a phone up there. And I want a squad car standing by." This to the operator. On with the black hat and out into the night, with Sergeant Panton at his heels.

13

They walked up to the farm. Quiet approach is good tactics, very often. Forewarned by the arrival of a car, the subject has time to be mentally prepared. Even to hide things. Faced quite suddenly with a grim-faced copper or two at the door, it is surprising what people will say or do. Especially if the house is full of goodies. So the inspector had no need to explain to the sergeant, who had done this sort of thing often enough, why they were keeping well in to the shadows, coming up the drive and into the cobbled yard.

Lights were on, in one upstairs room and the living room behind the French windows. Low down in the centre of the yellow rectangle marking the latter a small beam shone through, where the curtains had not been drawn properly to overlap. Still without need for speech the two policemen moved quietly forward, Rosher in the led. He bent down, to apply an eye. Sergeant Panton stood behind him, between the two urns filled with dying nasturtiums flanking two steps that led from the little crazy-pavement patio down to the yard proper. It's all still there. Quite a tourist attraction, nowadays.

It was a small chink. The inspector could not see the whole of the room. But he could see the twins. They stood at the table, doing something. He couldn't tell what, because whichever one had his back to the window was blocking the view, but it seemed to be engrossing them. He straightened up, stepping aside as he motioned to Sergeant Panton, telling him to take a look.

The sergeant bent. When he came up, Rosher jerked the black hat. They stepped softly to the far side of the patio. The inspector whispered: "Stay here. Watch 'em. I'm going to try the back door."

Dodgy, the sergeant thought. You'd better be able to pin something on 'em, if you're doing an illegal entry. We haven't got a warrant, we can land right in it. The inspector was whispering on:

"I want to know what they do, if I sing out from inside."

The sergeant nodded. That wasn't so bad. Nobody can nail you for opening the back door and singing out cheerily anybody home? So long as your feet stay on the mat. If it causes guilty starts and scurrying, the householder is probably bent. Having a watcher to see what is whisked away and to where can save a lot of time, and even the always maddening frustration of having the evidence vanished while you are applying for a warrant. Many and many a little rogue escapes like that, chortling as he goes.

Rosher crept away, prowling bandy into the murk. The whole world smelled of dying vegetable matter. The sergeant moved back over wet leaves come since Old Ossie cleaned the place up, to bend again at the little chink.

Still he could not make out what they were doing there. He could see this end of the table, which was draped in a fringe-bordered cloth; but his view was blocked still by the back of one brother, the other glimpsed only when he moved at the other side of the table. From this low angle his head only could be seen; and it, like that of the other, was bent forward. They were working at something, that was for sure. And it was keeping them quiet, they were doing no talking.

Rosher crept back. He jerked the hat again. Sergeant Panton moved to the edge of the patio. "Locked," Rosher whispered. Concentrated now. A good copper, come again into his true element and feeling the fierce hunter's joy rising. The sergeant stood as his brother. Adrenalin was lifting his blood, too. "I'm going to the front door. Right?"

The sergeant raised a thumb. No sense in more talk than is

138

necessary. Rosher crept away. The young man went back to his window.

When Rosher knocked on the door the effect sent that adrenalin leaping in sympathy through the sergeant's veins. Why he should knock instead of ringing the chime is moot. Some latent sense of drama, perhaps. Or possibly a man of combatative instincts all keyed for action automatically biffs the knocker rather than fiddle about finding the bell push. He certainly knocked, and sent a clap of pulse-stopping proportion thundering through the quiet house.

The twins shot upright: stood rigid for a long second with their heads turned to the door. Sergeant Panton saw shock—alarm—widening the only visible eyes: those of the twin facing him, in view now that both were upright. Then Rosher knocked again, a thunder as before.

They glanced at each other; began to scrabble together the something on the table. Then the one facing moved toward the passage leading to the front door; and the sergeant thought, exultantly: you clever old bugger! Look at 'em—look at 'em—you crafty old sod.

The twin with his back to the window turned now. He carried a small tray, with what seemed to be a tea caddy on it, and a small pair of scales. He came to the end of the table and jerked back the fringed cloth; which meant that he let go of the tray with one hand. It tilted. The sergeant saw a lot of small, square plastic bags, two of which fell to the floor. In a great hurry the youth pulled open the cutlery drawer at the table's end and shoved the tray in. He stopped and picked up the two fallen packets, fumbling in his haste.

Drugs, thought Sergeant Panton, excitement beating up in him. What else can it be? Christ—here's a turnup for the book. He'd been told nothing of Ossie's false notes; so he thought: is *that* what we're here for? And then again: Christ! Because the young man's hand came out from the drawer clutching a pistol. An automatic, which he shoved into the pocket of his jacket before closing the drawer, twitching the tablecloth back into place. And now he stood facing along the table, to where his brother had vanished out of the sergeant's vision.

It came to Sergeant Panton now that he didn't know what he should do. The rumble of Inspector Rosher's voice, an answering lighter tone had ceased at the front door, out of sight from here, around the corner. Presumably the inspector was already inside, coming along the passage toward this room.

Should he shout? Should he warn Rosher? The old bugger made a big thing about being horned in on. When I want your help I'll ask for it. That's what he said, Old Blubbergut barking. Famous for it.

But: a gun. Maybe he should shout. Shout, "Watch it—he's got a gun."

It might confuse Rosher—he might go for the wrong one— and if that bastard meant to use it, shock him and he might drag it out, start shooting.

The other bastard might have one.

So don't shout. You'll be in the steaming if you spark off shooting and the old sod gets it.

But you can't get in to help, can you? You'd have to smash through the glass—the window's locked, you tried it.

Too late now, anyway.

The inspector and the second twin had entered. Beyond the sergeant's sightline, he heard the gruff, half-barking voice say: "Good evening," and the lad with the gun's quiet reply.

"I'm here about a rather grave matter," Rosher said. "I'd like to know what you know about this." He was displaying the note. Unable to see, the sergeant thought: about what, for Christ's sake?

The out-of-sight twin spoke: "Why? What should we know about it?"

"It's a forgery, sir. I understand you gave it to somebody in the village."

If this came as a surprise to Sergeant Panton, it must have hit the twins like a sudden rush of brick, they with their minds on drugs rather than forgeries. Panton saw his twin's eyes flicker; and the other answered: "Us? Not us. Why should we give away five pound notes?"

Five pound note? The sergeant thought. What five pound note? He was slipping his shoes off. He'd try the door—perhaps they hadn't closed it. If he was inside, he could have that gun before they knew he was there. But silently—a scrape on cobbles or in the passage would alert them. A creep—a leap.

Rosher seemed to be going off at a tangent. He was saying: "What have you done with what was on the table? Shoved it out of sight somewhere, have you?"

Truth is, he believed the lads might have been sorting out funny money. They could have been doing something entirely innocent, of course; but if so, where were the materials? Innocence would have left them on the table, the twin not answering the door should still have been relaxed and probably working, not standing there stiffly, the cloth barren. By Christ, he could be onto something big.

It was, of course, bigger than he realised. Had he known drugs were involved he might have given a thought to guns. But his mind was fixed on forgery. And kudos. One little corner of his mind was gloating already: ho ho—two fingers to bloody Scotland Yard. This'd have the Old Man beaming.

The twins' compatible minds were spinning in a different direction, as Sergeant Panton sprinted in his nylon socks for the front door. They had been thinking primarily of drugs. This sudden introduction of a funny fiver shook them badly—they'd had no idea that any were around the village, loose. But in the cellar, on a shelf above dampness, was the bundle left to be dried when Simon took off on delivery; and the table drawer was stuffed with junk—which the old gorilla seemed to have seen them packaging. They reacted as their mother, upstairs out of the way, could have told him they always did to any hint of trouble or opposition: the hawk-like look coming down on their faces, their bodies drawn up arrogantly. But they said nothing.

The front door was shut. Sergeant Panton tugged the knob;

turned to sprint back to the patio. He should, perhaps, have rung the bell. A soft chime is not like a sudden shout. Somebody might have answered, if they were playing innocent, and he'd be in.

Ah well—hindsight is easy. In stockinged feet on a murky night, bemused by not having been put fully into the picture, a man making decisions does not necessarily make the right ones. And who is to say he made the wrong one? It wouldn't be the twin known to have a gun who came to the door, he was farthest from it. And the other might shout, slam the door, they might both start shooting. Or hold Rosher as hostage.

No—the sergeant cannot be blamed for what happened.

Inspector Rosher was looking at the lads, and feeling the uprising of his burly contempt. It did not pay, to stare hawklike at Rosher, whether you had parked on a double yellow or murdered your wife and all her unspeakable relatives. People had tried it, they had glared, they had tried to brow-beat, a very foolish few had even turned violent. One and all regretted it, later; and many were very much harder than two punk youths who were poisoning their mother. The tough ones could make him angry. For the twins he felt only contempt. He said, as Sergeant Panton began his silent return sprint: "I don't suppose there's a drawer in the end of that table, is there? I don't suppose you shoved it all in there."

A fair guess. Nowhere else so handy, given that the table had a drawer; and most old-fashioned dining tables do. Long experience told the inspector that the bent surprised in their bentness will rattle the gear under the nearest cover. And the cloth at the far end of the table had a kink in it. He hadn't noticed that, when he peered through the chink. He doubted it had been there.

But the speech added further shock to the twins' mind. The bastard knew it all—he knew. He was moving forward—confidently—he was going to open the drawer—

Sergeant Panton was back on the patio, bent with his eye to the chink. He saw Inspector Rosher come into view on the far side of the table, moving in the direction of the twin who had the pistol. He saw the lad's hand go into his pocket and come out to point the wicked thing straight at Rosher. He saw the inspector check, and heard him say without any apparent alarm, not barking but almost like an exasperated parent: "Now don't be a silly boy." He did not hear either twin say anything at all.

Why would they? Nothing they needed to say. They were done for, it was the moment when the weaker bent say all right, guv, it's a fair cop. The moment when the violent turn violent. Two bent minds confirming each other in their arrogance, with neither time nor desire to think of consequences beyond the present; with an instinctive urge to destroy what thwarted them and a blind belief that they, being special, would be all right—there is danger.

Christ! thought Sergeant Panton. Jesus! Diversion! He shaped to shoulder-charge the window. Thought: no—you'll cut yourself to bits, he'll get shot—*you'll* get shot. He looked around, hearing Inspector Rosher say in a very firm tone: "Give me that, lad. You'll only make it worse for yourself."

Almost before he finished speaking the sergeant was across the patio, and he was a strong young man. He picked up one of the urns, raised it above his head and sent it smashing through the window, nasturtiums and all. Admittedly, a plastic urn is not all heavy; but this one was filled with earth.

At the crash of glass, the billowing of the curtain, the twin's head turned; and Rosher dived into action. In a sense he had the advantage. He knew Sergeant Panton was out there, had expected something to happen. He'd have used the lad's guts, supposing he lived to do it, to strap up his boxy-toed shoes had he not done something. Now he dived, low; and the gun went off above his head as he took the twin at the knees.

The bullet smashed into the other twin's mouth, smashed through the lips, the teeth, the gums; came out through the spine to bury itself in the far wall as the lad threw up his hands, made one choking cry and dropped as Sergeant Panton, cursing cruelly, kicked out lower glass to force a way in through the window, and Inspector Rosher, scrambled already astride the fallen body of the lad with the gun, swept the Mighty Hammer down. The Hammer that in his day of glory sent so many men to sleep, huddled on canvas as this one slept now, on a very decent Wilton carpet.

The sergeant came crashing in. Rosher began to rise to his feet. Normally he was scrupulous in removing the black hat when he came into a house, but not when the occupants had been naughty. So firmly did it ride, low on the simian brow, that it had scarcely moved. Nevertheless, he resettled it, and said sternly: "What kept you?"

"I thought—I didn't—" said Sergeant Panton, his nylon socks all wet.

The inspector was not listening. He was producing the silver cuffs, to place on the wrists of the slumbering twin at his feet. "I want that car up here," he said, "and an ambulance. Not that it'll do much good, the other bugger's dead."

14

This was sensation. Hutton Fellows was knee-deep in press-men—the first arrived almost before poor Mrs. Wellington departed to the cottage hospital, where she lay now, still doped and boozed into a coma—and up to the buttocks in cars and rubber-necks after the telly news. They saw very little, the police having a guard stationed at the end of the drive and others scattered about the fields and other points of entry. They grumbled, these rubber-necks, and their children whined; but all were comforted somewhat by a mobile opportunist who set up his van and did a fair trade in hamburgers, hot dogs and toffee apples, far into the night.

Inspector Rosher was seen again on television, but briefly, standing with Chief Superintendent Bishop and Sergeant Panton against the background of the station; but this time he had a non-speaking part, the super doing the talking. Less said to the press by those directly involved in the shooting, the better. There is always somebody waiting to pounce and stir it for the police, when somebody dies.

As always when something suddenly blows up, there was not much sleep for anybody at the station that night. The Chief Superintendent was in, and looking worried. Scotland Yard men were on the way again, to deal with the notes found in the cellar, and the Drugs Squad moved in to take charge of the other matter. Plenty of activity, but none of it related to murder. And none of it seeming likely to lead much further, in the immediate future. This because of one unfortunate factor. The devastating Hammer attached to the hairy arm of Inspector Rosher.

It shattered the twin's jaw. He, too, lay in the cottage hospital not far from where his mother snored, wired up and sedated, having collapsed completely when he woke up to find his brother dead. In self-defense the inspector had to tap him again, which put another crack in his jaw. Nobody even knew, at this stage, which twin he was. The point was academic, neither was in condition to talk.

Nobody blamed Rosher. A man with a gun on him must do the best he can. Even those—and they were many—who privately doubted whether the second clump was strictly necessary admitted to themselves that they'd have clipped the little bastard, too, with the sergeant in the hall phoning for an ambulance and no witnesses. Nevertheless, men began to avoid him, and the Chief Superintendent when he addressed him showed signs of embarrassment. This is not good.

Rosher himself was worried. He knew the truth of that second clump; but then, how was he to know the little sod had a glass jaw? He'd faced one disciplinary enquiry, he didn't want another. The unease set his features grimly, glittered in his eyes, brought out the Old Blubbergut so that men avoided him further, and thus increased his unease.

It was Sergeant Panton who came up with cause for a little action. He, too, was still at the station, and thinking about things, when an idea came to him. He sat down forthwith and telephoned his grass, the one called Clifford Baggin, who said: "Christ, Mr. Panton—it's bloody midnight. I went to bed early, I thought it was a bloody fire alarm."

"Something I want to know. You heard about the Wellington twins?"

"Yeah—it was on the news. What about it?" He sounded uneasy. Nothing unusual, your grass normally does.

"The Laughing Jackass the other night—they were with the Watson-Harvey girl. Did they go there often—all three of 'em together?"

146

"Well, Christ . . . I don't know, do I?"

"Come off it—you're in there all the time, you know everything that goes on. Don't sod me about, I'm in a hurry."

"Well, yeah. Once a week. Lately."

"Uh-huh. Same night every week?"

"Well, yeah."

"That was the only night?"

"Yeah."

Memory, jogged, was coming up now with things the sergeant did not know he had noticed, and certainly had not thought about. They'd been some time alone—she came out of the Ladies. "Did she always go into the bog? Straight off?"

"Christ, I wouldn't know, would I? I don't sit leering at 'em coming out of the bog—"

"I don't want to turn nasty with you, lad."

"All right, all right. Yes."

"Uh-huh. And other girls went in and out?"

"I . . . look, for Christ's sake, Mr. Panton, you can't expect me to give names—"

"All right, Willie—you're a good lad. Names don't matter, we'll gather 'em in."

Young Baggin knew it was drugs. He'd known what they were up to all along. He said urgently: "You won't lumber me, will you? For Christ's sake—" They call often upon Christ, the little bent. Well, he came to save sinners.

"Just keep your nose clean, we'll see you're all right." The sergeant hung up, leaving another night's repose utterly ruined, and went to see his superiors.

Ten minutes later he left again for Hutton Fellows, with an inspector from the drugs squad and a lady sergeant. "We won't call on you this time, Mr. Rosher," the Chief Constable said. "You've had a long day, I suggest half an hour with the feet up."

There were problems, of course, at the Watson-Harvey house. Mr. Watson-Harvey, in a plaid dressing gown, came to the door and let them in before he realised they had come for his daughter, sharing her mother's bed because of her condition. Fiona went again into hysterics at sight of them, while Mother, when she knew what they had come for, screamed at them to get out and leave her baby alone.

The Drugs Squad inspector was equal to it all. He had seen too much pretty humanity wrecked by the stuff to have much sympathy for anybody suspected of running it about. For all he knew, Mum and Dad could be in it, too. "You have the choice," he snapped. "Your daughter can come voluntarily to assist us in our inquiries, or I can arrest her. And you, too, if you persist in obstructing me in the execution of my duty."

Even at this hour the village, not long in bed after sitting up to watch the late-news broadcasts and to discuss the wonderful day, lit up again like a Christmas tree as people shot out into front gardens or twitched curtains to watch as the police cars—a second one had to be commandeered from those around the Murder Wagon—rolled through the main street and over the bridge, bearing the entire Watson-Harvey family away.

Fiona had to be sedated again. The doctor's dose wore off long ago, and they half carried her into the station kicking and screaming. Which upset her mother no end. The poor lady was already halfway there, and when she learned that her lamb must go into a cell—there was debate as to whether she, too, should be moved to the cottage hospital—she went all the way, laughing, crying, screaming, throwing her arms about, until the doctor managed to jab her into somnolent quiet. She it was who went to hospital. Mr. Watson-Harvey, ashen-faced and shaking so that he could hardly hold the pen, was taken down with her in the police ambulance after signing little forms to say that whatever had been done was all right by him.

That concluded the entertainment for the day. A long day, stretching well into the small hours. Well. C.I.D. men are used to that, it goes with the salary. Some of them went home now: Fiona would not be awake and in command of her faculties for a long time yet, and as for the twins, God knew when they'd get at him. But the big fry stayed: the Chief Constable, to greet the Scotland

148

Yard men when they arrived; Chief Superintendent Bishop, who as officer in charge of a murder case that shot suddenly sideways had to be here at the side of Inspector Rosher and Sergeant Panton, who must set out clearly when they were all ensconsed in the Chief's panelled office exactly what happened at the Wellington farm. Their written reports were already in; but Scotland Yard would want verbals as well.

Dawn was not far off when the men from London suggested that they all go up to the farm; but the Chief Constable overruled this. "I will come," he said, "but these gentlemen have been on duty since early yesterday morning. They are engaged upon a murder case, one of them has been shot at." Both written reports emphasised that the gun had been pointed at Rosher. As it undoubtedly was. The Chief sat at his desk, weary enough himself but able to smile at his own family. "Go home, Mr. Bishop, Mr. Rosher, Sergeant. I shall phone if we need you."

One of the Scotland Yard men spoke with the slightly disparaging air marked only too often, alas, in the London special assignment man when his pointed pavement shoes take him beyond Watford Gap. "I don't suppose you get a lot of shooting around here."

The Chief's eye flashed cold. "Quite enough to satisfy us, thank you. Goodnight, Mr. Bishop—gentlemen. And thank you."

The break from duty was not a long one. It rarely is, once things begin to happen. It's the normal pattern: hiatus at the start of a case; sudden frenzied activity as everything comes at once. Inspector Rosher had time for a much needed clean-up, even a couple of hours in bed; but he got no sleep. However rugged a man, however limited in imagination, he cannot out of Hollywood dive under a blazing gun without disturbance afterwards, when the adrenalin is long gone and the blood sags and he thinks of what would have happened had he dived a split second later and a foot further up.

The veteran knows how to cope with this condition. He forces his mind away. This does not bring rest, but it steadies the unrest.

It can even be productive. Rosher had been fired upon before, as a highly spit-and-polished sergeant (Military Police) in the later of the World Wars and several times since. He applied his veteran discipline, and thought about his work.

Sod another Old Man's enquiry. This Old Man wasn't the old Old Man, who bust him down before; but sod another, so near retirement. He was lucky to be in line for full pension—he refused to let his mind run around retirement, it was the one thing that frightened him—and even with the Old Man on his side (and he was, thank Christ, up to now), to be the subject of *any* enquiry left a blot on the book. To be subject of two—dicey. Very dicey.

But he didn't regret banging the little bastard again. Shot at him, didn't he? And then went berserk when he came to. Yes, yes, agreed, it would have been fairly easy to pin him, he had the cuffs on—but if ever a little bastard needed banging! He hurled himself, foaming and screaming, kicking, biting. And a man needs a little pleasure from his work.

It probably wouldn't come to anything. Young Panton wasn't there, and he hated the little sods anyway. For his, Rosher's money, they'd be found to have done the Nolan character—the girl hinted at it, to the doctor—and the Poddy lad, too. Drugs in him, weren't there? And they were into drugs, the girl and all. All in together, most likely. Fell out about it. That note on young Poddy's pad: blackmail—

Or written on behalf of all? A consignment that didn't arrive? Sparked off a split—all in the forgery caper, too. . . .

His eyes were closing; thought was fogging. The telephone jerked him back. He rolled out of bed and padded through his dust-and-clutter living room, clutching his pyjama trousers to prevent their falling down, out to the hall and his only telephone. The hall clock said nine-thirty. So did his wristwatch. He had no reason to doubt them, they were none of your modern digitals that suddenly spin like fruit machines.

It was the Archbishop. He said: "The station just rang. Sergeant Noakes has been sitting with the Watson-Harvey girl, she's a good girl." He meant Sergeant Noakes, blonde and quite pretty but for crooked teeth. And his tone of avuncular approval said that male chauvanism is not dead yet, by any means. Not in police forces. "She's come to, much quieter. Our girl's been talking to her, she does that sort of thing very well, that's why I had her in there. She says the girl is ready to chat. I'm just going down."

"I'll be right there," said Rosher.

The Archbishop made a plummy little pleasantry. "Don't break your neck. You've got time to button your flies."

No time for the soap-and-brush shave which Rosher preferred, though. A quick run around the stubble with his electric razor, a scrub at the big brown teeth and a quick mug of biting-black tea to wash down the slice of bread and marmalade, and he was in the car and on the way. Two pressmen met him in the station reception area, and he made a smile for them because it is well to keep in with the press; but he kept travelling, saying: "Sorry—no comment," on along the clacking corridor to where Chief Superintendent Bishop waited, in his office. Cutting corners off his toilette got him here first: he was fingering his chin with one hand, battery razor in the other. Bishop said:

"Can't get a decent shave with these things. Never could, you need a lather. Right—if you're ready?"

They went together along the corridor and down the stone steps to the stone passage, which is kept warm enough by ugly old radiators and pipes that go clunk in the night, but always feels chilly. There is only earth under, of course, they say that's what does it. Fiona lay under blankets in the narrow cell bunk, the quite pretty Sergeant Noakes beside her.

"Good morning, Sergeant," said Superintendent Bishop.

"Good morning, sir." The sergeant showed her crooked teeth.

The Archbishop turned to the girl. Quiet, yes; and ill-looking. Violet shadows under the enormous, feverish eyes and hair not straggled—somebody had been at it with a comb, probably the sergeant, all girls together—but greasy-looking, dull where it used to be shining. Fastened back with pins, almost the old-fashioned Holloway-prisoner style. She gazed at them with a sort of dumb terror, still not clear entirely of the sedatives, perhaps; worn out by too great hysteria. The superintendent smiled upon her, saying like an uncle: "Well now, miss—I believe you have something to tell us."

The great eyes flicked sideways, seeking Sergeant Noakes; a look of desperation, a need for her friend. "It's all right, dear." The sergeant smiled reassuringly, spoke gently. "Just tell the gentleman what you told me." She reached, to hold and pat the reaching hand.

"Yes. Yes," Fiona said. Whispering, like a lately beaten and terrified child. "What . . . what . . . do you want to know?"

"Let's start at the beginning, shall we?" the super suggested, soothingly. "Right at the beginning. We could do with another chair in here. Mr. Rosher, would you mind seeing to it?"

It took half an hour to get the full story out of her, she clinging to Sergeant Noakes's hand the whole time. She told of the man peddling drugs around the college; of how she told the twins, who came back to her afterwards suggesting a meeting with the man. Of an arrangement made—she didn't know the details, they shoved her aside—of the weekly trips to the Laughing Jackass for dancing and passing out little packets. Teddy Poddy was in it somewhere—she didn't know where, but it was something to do with selling. Neither she nor the twins knew that Teddy was mentally unstable when they let him in—he was a friend of hers—they found out later.

She did not mention that she, after a wild and hilarious time when he seemed excitingly different and vibrant—schizophrenics often do, in the high times—as well as handsome, found out the hard way when he cried that he was God and she the Devil, and he was going to kill her for her own good as soon as he finished what he was doing: to wit, straddling her in the Wellington's barn. She got out from under and away. Lucky girl.

Tom Nolan, she said, appeared during Teddy's sojourn in hospital. Again, she did not know all the details; but she gathered that Teddy, in his high, had told Nolan the entire set-up. Nolan, out of hospital, more or less forced his way in, using blackmail. At first he demanded only a regular supply, presumably for himself;

152

but something happened—last week—she wasn't told what, whether he increased his demands, for money or more drugs or what—she didn't know—but a meeting was arranged. She was there, they said they'd want her there.

(She did not say why they should; but the policemen had no doubt. A girl in no position to refuse can offer or be coerced into offering services which to a young unbalanced rogue sleeping alone and rough, can be desirable enough to deflect him, at least temporarily, from his original purpose. She could buy them time, which would be useful while they decided what to do about him. That—or they had already decided, and wanted her there to bind her even tighter in silence, as accessory.)

This was three days before Teddy's death. No, she didn't know if Nolan had seen Teddy since he came out. Mrs. Wellington—they were bastards—oh, they were bastards—(Sergeant Noakes held her hand tight)—was in bed, they'd given her pills and stuff—they were killing her—and Nolan, when he arrived, became overexcited and said he wouldn't talk about anything while she was there. He said you can't trust any woman. So she went into the living room with Timothy, while he and Simon stayed in the kitchen. And soon after, she heard a bump and a cry.

They went back into the kitchen, where Tom Nolan was on the floor and Simon was standing with one of the shotguns in his hands, held by the barrel. He said Tom attacked him and he hit him in self-defence. With the butt.

Then they sent her home. No—she didn't know what they'd done with Tom, they told her later it would be all right. She didn't know if they killed Teddy, too—but she thought they probably did. "They killed Rover," she said. "They shot him . . . they shot Rover—" And here the dulled edge sharpened again. The Holloway head rocked on the thin, beautiful neck, the delicate, manicured hands went up to cover the face; in an agony of sudden weeping she wailed: "They shot my Rover. . . . They killed my dog—"

Chief Superintendent Bishop sat, impassively. Inspector Rosher stood, having brought in only one of the little wooden chairs. Sergeant Noakes looked down at her hands; folded them in her lap, biting her lips. They waited until the girl quieted; and then the superintendent said, quite gently: "We won't press you any further now, miss. We shall be seeing you again." To charge you, to take your statement down. To gather details of your contacts.

The girl looked at him, stained and wet with tears. "Will I . . . do you . . . have to tell Mummy and Daddy?"

Jesus Christ, Rosher thought, startled. You'd think she was a bloody infant, broken a playground window.

The Archbishop was saying: "Your mother is in the hospital at present. Nothing serious, just upset. Your father is—we will make arrangements for visiting."

"No," she said. "No—I can't see them. . . ."

"Now, now, now," said the rather pretty sergeant.

The superintendent got up from his chair. Inspector Rosher shifted his weight, preparing to leave. Mr. Bishop said: "Have they brought your breakfast? We feed you, you know."

Fiona looked up at him; spoke in her childish whisper. "What . . . what will happen to me?"

"You'll be going to prison, sweetheart, I expect," the super said benignly. "You'll be going to prison. For a very long time."

Strange, really, she being so closely involved; but in all the world for miles around—you could say, in the whole of the nation—she was about the only person in reasonable health come to the age of understanding the printed word, the broadcast voice, the television news, who did not know that one of the twins was dead. And they had not yet pressed her on the matter—it was enough, to keep her talking—but neither did she seem to know anything about the forgery caper.

The super said, at the door: "I suppose you are also party to the passing of forged notes?"

"What notes?" she said; and a solid policeman knows, at a time of confession, the lack of interest that spells ignorance. No flick in the eyes, no sudden guard; and anyway, having confessed so much, why deny this?

So the two men came out from the cell, leaving the lady sergeant to deal with the girl as she saw fit, always within the laid-down code of conduct; and as they clacked up from dungeon level into the clacking corridor they met the Chief Constable, with his hat and coat on. Poor man, he'd been up *all* night. The Scotland Yard men gave the farm a true working over, without discovering anything new. He took them to their hotel, had breakfast with them, and went home. As he sank sighing into bed, curtains drawn against the light, the telephone rang. Here he was, bug-eyed but game to the last. He said: "Ah—good morning, gentlemen. I imagine you are coming from Miss Watson-Harvey. Any joy?" A strange choice of expression, there is not much joy in underground cells.

"Confession, sir," said Mr. Bishop. "Drugs involvement—the Nolan murder—she seems to be accessory."

"Mm. Mm. Used to know her father. Shall we go up to my office?" The headman led the way. When the Archbishop had summarised what transpired downstairs, he said: "Terrible. Terrible thing for the parents. I knew them, you know, he used to play scrum half." A deep, deep sigh. "Good work, Mr. Bishop. You'll be getting a list of her contacts, of course."

"When we take her written statement, sir. No point in leaning on her just now, it might send her off again."

"Of course. Mm. The Drugs Squad should be happy. What about the forgery business?"

"I don't think she's mixed up in that, sir. They seem to have operated it independently."

"Mm. Well, that's the Yard's pigeon. And you feel these Wellingtons are also responsible for the Poddy lad?"

"It seems pretty open and shut, sir, yes."

"Yes. Yes. Well—very good work, gentlemen. You will keep me in the picture, of course, Mr. Bishop?" His dismissal phrase. No need for it, beyond the courteous implication that the other man does it of his courtesy. God help the investigating officer who does not keep his Chief in the picture. The lesser men were at the door when the big one spoke again, almost diffidently. "Oh—Mr. Rosher . . . just a word, if I may."

155

The Archbishop shot a quick glance sideways at Rosher, and went on out of the room. The Chief said: "The . . . er . . . Wellington lad, the one we have. He did have the cuffs on, the second time you had to . . . mm . . . restrain him?"

"Yes, sir," said Rosher. His whole bearing had stiffened and the voice verged on his bark. "He became violent. It's in my statement."

"Yes," the Chief said. "Yes. Mm. Only I've had a call from the hospital. Apparently he is not pulling round at all. Not responding. Lying in a sort of coma. He seems to be Timothy, by the way. We had his aunt taken in. Mrs. Poddy. She's not sure— he's swollen, of course, and wired up and so on—but she thinks he's Timothy. Sinking, is what they said."

"Uh-huh." Head thrust forward slightly, little eyes suspiciously glittering, never did the inspector look more as if he belonged, not in a close-carpeted and panelled office but up a suitably stout tree, wondering if he should mangle David Attenborough.

"Shock, of course. Terrible shock, for a twin to wake up and find he's killed his brother. They were, apparently, very close. Inseparable. That sort of thing has been known to . . . er . . . cause sinking. Decline. You didn't hit the gun? Knock it aside, as you dived at him, deflect the bullet? Anything of that nature?"

"I went under it, sir." And nearly got my bloody head blown off. "It's all in the statement." Rosher was doing the thing men dreaded. He was producing his great grey handkerchief. Deliberately grey, this one, he had learned that if you buy grey ones they stay clean much longer. The Chief spoke hastily.

"Yes. Well, thank you, Mr. Rosher. Thank you. That will be all."

Too late. The handkerchief was at the hairy nostrils. The Chief braced himself, settling the head somewhat between the elegant shoulders.

15

Around lunchtime, in the persons of Inspector Rosher and Sergeant Panton, the police paid a call upon Timothy Wellington, they believed it was. Word came in from the uniform branch man doing guard at his bedside, to say that he had lapsed into total unconsciousness and the hospital people were worried. "You go, Mr. Rosher," said Chief Superintendent Bishop. Never on first-name terms with Rosher, he had suddenly become very formal. "I'll deal with the girl's statement and so on, and do the press conference. There are reporters down in reception. Be circumspect."

Could it have been that he preferred not to be too closely identified with Rosher, under present circumstances; that he felt the presence of that man at the conference might attract awkward questions which he would find difficulty in fending off, constrained by having him here? Could be. You never know, do you? He may have had word from Upstairs.

Timothy, if it was he, certainly looked very sick. Wired up and bandaged, wax-skinned, unmoving, he lay in a private cubicle with his eyes closed. Yes, in view of the situation you may speak to him, the doctor said. Not that it will do much good. Normally I would not allow it. And do it quietly—no badgering, no attempt to bully him awake, I'm not prepared to answer for the consequences.

Rosher spoke to the lad quietly. The doctor was right, it did no good. Timothy continued to lie supine, tucked in very neatly with his lashes surprisingly long and soot-dark against the wax skin. "I'm afraid you won't get any answer," the doctor said.

"Er-rrmph," said Rosher. "When do you think he'll be . . . er . . . *compis mentis*?"

"I'm not at all sure that he will. Not uncommon, you know—twin brothers, completely identified with each other from the womb—plenty of documented cases. And this one apparently shot his alter ego. Might as well have shot himself."

"Uh-huh." The inspector's face was grimly set, brows low and eyes hard. Bit of a bastard for him, Sergeant Panton thought, with his past history. And it wasn't his fault. Well—the first part wasn't. "Are you saying he might die?"

"One way or the other," the doctor said, "you could say he's already dead."

The inspector cleared his throat. "Thank you, doctor. I'll leave my sergeant here, if I may, just in case. Sergeant Panton, you'll stay here. Get on to me immediately, if there's any change."

"Right, sir," said the sergeant. Might as well toss him a sir, cheer the poor old bugger up a bit.

Inspector Rosher moved away, accompanied by the doctor. In the passage leading back to Reception—he had nearly met his own end in that passage, not long ago. Another, classier villain with a gun—he asked after Mrs. Wellington and Fiona's mother. Not because he was burning to know how they were, and there was no point in visiting either; but back at the station they would expect that he would ask and perhaps faintly raise an eyebrow if he did not. When trouble gathers, neglect nothing.

"Mrs. Watson-Harvey will be going home today," the doctor told him. "Mrs. Wellington will be here for some time, of course. We may have to transfer her to a nursing home later. But she is comfortable. Quite comfortable." And she probably was. She would not yet have been told about her sons, she could still have been floating in blissful limbo.

"Uh-huh," said Rosher. "Thank you, doctor. Good day." He went through the glass door, bandying rapidly down the steps and into the car. Somewhere in the building was a pretty West Indian nurse, the one who looked after him when he lay in a condition much less comfortable than the one Mrs. Wellington was said to be in. He might have called to say hallo—he thought of doing so. But it would only stir up the erotic dreams in which she vied already for top billing over the brothel madam who had held the position for a long time now. He slammed himself into the car—not his own, he culled one from the official pool. Too short a trip for worthwhile profit—and said: "Sod it." He then began to climb out again.

Sergeant Panton came down the steps, approaching at the half run. "Sorry," he said, handing them over. "Forgot to give you the keys."

"Grrmph," said Rosher. And now he could drive away; back to the station, which he entered through the C.I.D. room at the side to avoid Superintendent Bishop's press conference, still going on. Unlike him, to shun the press, with whom he got on well. They liked him because he was a character, and characters make copy. He did not like them; but humanity enjoys its name in lights, and official policy calls for cooperation. To heck with official policy today, though—he might have had his bellyful of the press, in the near future. He dodged, and from his office called Sergeant Barney Dancey, in the glassed-in box of a reception office. Barney would ring back, to tell him when the Archbishop was free.

Ten minutes before the intercom buzzed, during which he sat at his desk thinking deep. Barney Dancey said: "Alf? Archie just finished. He's on his way to his office." All men were first name to this good man.

"Ta, Barney," the inspector said. A flip of the switch, up with his bottom from the chair, and he was on his way to make report to Superintendent Bishop, who reciprocated when he had received it.

"Mm. Well, I think we can count the Nolan case as cleared. The girl's made her statement and signed it. I've told the press. She doesn't know anything about the forgery lark, that's obvious. But that's Scotland Yard's headache, really, they're in with her now. She still doesn't want to see her father. When he comes in

I'll have a word with him. We'd better acquaint him with the full extent of the charges, prepare him a bit before he goes in."

"Shall I give him a ring?"

"No. Better to do it face to face. He's got a plateful, at the moment. He rang earlier—I couldn't give permission for him to come in then."

"What about the Poddy caper?"

"Mm. That's a bit in the air, until we can speak to your young man." *If* we can speak to your young man, before they lay him beside his brother on a slab. "The girl clearly wasn't in on that, but I think we're justified in assuming they did him, too. No doubt that will clarify itself when we get dug into the drugs caper. The twins could have been acting under orders, you know what the syndicates are. Two little operators step out of line—eliminate them." The super was speaking as though he came up against the syndicates every day. He didn't, of course. Not in this town. "I reckon they were acting in cahoots—both a bit out of kink, and friends—cooked up a plan between them—blackmail, probably, the note suggests it. They weren't dyed-in-the-wool pros, they wouldn't have known what they were getting into." The longer the Archbishop talked, the more ecclesiastic became his tone. He positively pomped, sitting back with fingers steepled. "Altogether, we're not coming out of it too badly. I've been on the blower to the Old Man. He seems very pleased. And the press are happy, I've fed them."

Rosher was feeling a small relief. The hook was by no means prised from his gullet; but to have clonked a known killer in the process of arrest is a different matter from clonking a suspect and—it would be more than suggested if the press took off—causing him to slaughter his brother. Editors and do-gooders make more capital out of the villain damaged than they do out of the copper shot. "Uh-huh," he said, and got up to go.

It was quiet, in his own office. Hardly had he sat down at his desk and arranged his scowl for thinking than a knock brought Inspector Young Alec Cruse. He said: "Your bank idea seems to have turned a little something up. The account the money came out of was Barclays, Honnerton Street."

"Where's that?"

"In the city."

"Took a bit of time come up, didn't it?"

"Nothing matched first time round. We couldn't get all the tellers' dabs. People go sick, things like that, or they're off duty, having a pee, gone for coffee—you know. We sent another wave in, and there's the match." The young man proferred two photostat copies of two identical fingerprints, blown up big. "Mrs. Joan Couldwell, the teller. They have little plates with their names on, at Barclays."

"Mr. Bishop seen 'em?"

"He's just gone out. Want me to raise him?"

"No. Leave it with me. Got the bank's number?"

"Switchboard'll get it."

"Uh-huh. Right. Thanks."

Away went Inspector Young Alec. Rosher reached for his phone. A plug was inserted here and there, a directory was riffled, modern technology jigged and clicked into action, bringing the voice of the bank manager into his ear. Rosher told who he was, explained what he wanted. The bank manager said: "I am sorry, I cannot give details of customers' private accounts. We have a strict ruling."

"I don't need details," Rosher said. "I just want to know who has an account and has been making large withdrawals. Or one large withdrawal."

"Impossible. We are in the middle of a business area. Many of our customers make large withdrawals."

"A list of 'em would do. Those paid out by Mrs. Joan Could-well. You keep records."

"Quite out of the question. Our only records are on the computer, we don't list our clerks individually. You don't know what you're asking. Besides—over the telephone? I don't even know you are who you say you are."

"Mm. You could ring me back here, at the station. The switchboard will confirm."

"No, no, no. I'm sorry—no, no. There is nothing I can do to help you. Certainly not over the telephone."

Well, Rosher had half expected it. More than half, even the police cannot simply ring and demand details of a bank customer's private affairs. But a phone call serves to prepare the ground. He said: "I quite understand that, sir. Very commendable. Perhaps I can call in to see you. The inquiry is rather serious."

"I am available. But I am afraid I shall need very much higher authority before I can do anything of this nature."

End of conversation. Putting the phone back on its bracket, Rosher thought: might as well go over. Leave word for Archie Bishop. I need to get out, do something. It's not as though I battered the little sod's head in with a truncheon, all I did was show him the Hammer.

Now policemen do not give much trust to inspiration. They prefer to plod. Outside the detective novel inspiration is deeply mistrusted, cases are cleared on the soles of the feet. Nevertheless it has to be agreed that a detective over the arduous years develops a sort of antenna-sensitivity; and, as an artist works best under pressure, so does your policeman sometimes respond with mental agility beyond his normal working scope, when he is largely concerned with personal stresses.

In Rosher now, the mental jump was without doubt related to his stress. In a police force, results count. Given results sufficiently weighty, the little problem in the other scale-pan goes right up in the air, to be quietly removed and pushed down the nearest plug-hole. Not only in police forces is it ever thus.

The blackmail angle tickled Rosher's antenna. It didn't quite fit. Young Poddy used that odd, quasi-playful endearment. He wouldn't have addressed the twins like that, would he? Addressing the twins, at least it would have been in the plural.

Well, he wouldn't have been addressing the twins, would he? If the blackmail money came out of their account, they handled it in gloves. Their prints were on file now—but they didn't appear on the notes.

Somebody else. One of the syndicate? Who passed it on to the higher-up, who ordered the twins to rub him out?

Well—no. Because they wouldn't stab him and leave him unburied in the woods. Nolan, yes—a grave had been found for him. He'd have been in it yet if the floods hadn't washed him out. Forensic said he'd been buried, and the water-damaged hole was obviously where he'd been.

Of course, it didn't have to be drugs. He could have got wind of the funny-money lurk, he might have been in on it. As for the note: not much help, it could have been addressed to anybody, anywhere in the country. He was as bent as they were, it could have related to some other matter entirely, nothing to do with them. Bent, he'd probably got things going on the side.

It didn't quite fit, it made static in his receiver. He had donned the black hat and the battleship-grey raincoat, left his office and clacked all the way to the reception hall on his way out when it occurred to him that for a blackmail victim to pay out on the scale young Poddy had tapped in for, he had to be pretty well-to-do. And to be vulnerable, he must have something to hide. There was only one rich man in the vicinity of this case. The man with the big house and the beautiful women.

The man who, surprisingly, had not been in personally as yet, to visit the daughter sitting in a cell.

Surprising. Why would a man not be in? A man who, when last seen, was wracked with concern for his women.

No: more positively: why would such a man keep away?

Surprising. Suspicious? The inspector turned 'round and clacked all the way back again, the length of the corridor and down the stone steps to where the air strikes chilly in spite of the thunking radiators.

Fiona looked a little better. Her hair was still somewhat flattened, but it seemed to be rousing itself and her eyes were more directly focused. Such beautiful eyes—the envy of her friend the lady sergeant, who sat with her still and, being uniform branch, could afford a few pots of mascara and a set of lashes out of the overtime. The C.I.D. gets nothing, however long it works. Inspector Rosher, let in, said:

"Your father, miss. He's pretty well-to-do?"

The girl looked surprised. When you are sitting in a cell on drugs charges, this kind of question you do not expect. "Well . . . yes," she said. "Yes, I expect he is."

"What is his line of business, exactly?"

"Well . . . he's got the family firm—and the two furniture stores—and . . . I don't know, he's director of some things. And the printers."

"Printers?"

"That's only a little one. Teddy used to work for him there."

"Uh-huh. Right." Without let or hindrance, the inspector turned and left. The cell door clonked shut behind him, the rattle of keys mingled with his clacking as he walked away.

He spent the next half hour back in his office, with the city business directory; but first he called upon Sergeant Barney Dancey in Reception, and on the fingerprint boys. He never did get to the bank; but then, after that small flash of inspiration he had no need to.

The fingerprint lads did an excellent job. When they delivered the result, he pressed the switch on his intercom and spoke again to Sergeant Barney. "Archie back yet?"

"Five minutes ago. He's in his office."

Up got the inspector and trod yet again along the passage, bearing his pieces of paper and the directory. The adrenalin was pumping in him now. One in the eye here for Scotland Yard? It could be—it could be. And the out-of-town copper who dots the eye of Scotland Yard amasses kudos where it counts, gaining the close-mouthed goodwill of his pleased colleagues—and of his Chief Constable, who will certainly see to it that no more is said about little side-troubles. It is the bush policeman's nagging fear that that Scotland Yard men may indeed be superior that makes him so happy to put them down.

164

Chief Superintendent Bishop heard his inspector through. Then he said: "Mmm. I admit, the blackmail angle doesn't sit too well with me. I've wondered if the whole lot of them were in that together—your twins, Nolan and Poddy."

"Maybe. It doesn't alter this, does it?" Rosher indicated his two photostats: one of a Nilhildrin-treated note, liberally endowed with fingerprints, one ringed; the other showing the form signed last night by Mr. Watson-Harvey. The superintendent, leaning back in his chair, was toying still with the magnifying glass that had shown him how neatly the two matched. "And his main place of business—the tea importing caper, where his office is—it's along Honnerton Street. Right by the bank."

"Granted. Mm. But you're leaping about a bit, don't you think? Nothing to connect him with anything, let alone the forgery business." And he's some kind of friend of the Old Man.

"Only his printing business. He's not listed as having one. Is he? The rest are here—import and export, tea importer, furniture stores, director of this and that—no printers. And where is he? Wouldn't you expect him to be in?"

"He's probably had his plate full with the wife." Both men knew that the senior rank was doing what it has to do: advancing points designed to test the high-flown theory, especially one with the suspect so close to the Top Dog. Both knew that it is funny, if an apparently devoted father does not hover demanding to see his imprisoned offspring; and maybe the presence of the Chief Constable if known to him, when he is denied. There is a pattern to these things. Any policeman knows it.

"Or he's afraid to come near. He won't know the twin's not talking—if he thinks he is, he'll be afraid we know all about it. He may even have scarpered."

"Wait a minute, wait a minute—it's too far up in the air. We can't arrest him. There's nothing to at all to connect him definitely with anything—"

"Except blackmail. And blackmail means he's bent." There were no shades of grey on Rosher's palette. Humanity was bent, or it was not. Mostly, it was.

The superintendent sat for a moment, considering. No senior rank can afford to reject out of hand any theory, however unlikely, brought to it by a seasoned colleague. For Rosher's limited qualities he had respect: and simply because the man *was* limited, and not known to leap about in the air, when he came with something straight off the antenna, the something could well contain substance. Certainly, if a subject is vulnerable to blackmail he has something to hide. So the super pulled his nose and went er-rr-rmph as he cleared his throat; and finally said: "I don't dispute that he must have something in his background that we might find ourselves looking into, but there's no connection whatever with the bent money."

"Except his printers."

"Which he may not have anymore. It's not a connection, there are millions of printers. Look, leave it with me for an hour, will you? Let me think about it. Come back to me and if it's standing up we'll take it up to the Old Man."

"Right," said Rosher. He could trust it with Archie.

By now, it was lunchtime. When he left the super's office he went up to the canteen and stolidly munched through a quantity of solid matter; without much appetite, but firm in his policeman's policy of eating while you can. He was washing it down with his second mug of rumbustious tea when an emissary arrived from Sergeant Barney Dancey. Would he care to have a word with Mr. Watson-Harvey, waiting in Reception?

Mr. Watson-Harvey was clearly under heavy stress. Only to be expected, considering all the circumstances. His face drawn and almost twitching, eyes feverish and dark in dark circles, he said harshly as soon as Rosher appeared: "I am told I cannot see my daughter. I *demand* to see her."

"Superintendent Bishop feels it would hamper us in our investigations, sir," the inspector said.

"How? I am her father. I demand—"

"If you will step this way, I'll see what I can do."

The inspector ushered the visitor into one of those small interview rooms adjoining Reception; thinking: lunchtime—and he's only just arrived. Without a solicitor. He said: "How is the wife, sir?"

"I am going to collect her. From the hospital. As soon as I have seen my daughter."

Here from fatherly affection? Or to find out what she's said? You'd be in the cell alone with her—is that why you didn't bring a solicitor? "I am afraid that won't be possible, just at the moment."

"Where is your Superintendent? I demand to see him."

Bluster? Genuine hysteria, born of stress and concern for his child all alone, being beaten with rubber truncheons? "Sit down, sir," the inspector said, indicating the hard little chair in front of a hard little desk. This was not the soothing interview room. This was sparse, and deliberately hostile. "If you'll wait a minute, I'll see if I can find him."

He left the man there and went straight to his office; came back with the file he had been working on. What he had in there was nebulous, bits of circumstantial conjecture. No proof of anything; except that this man handled the blackmail money. But he had the man—and no witnesses. When he re-entered the bare little room he said: "I'm afraid Mr. Bishop is out, sir."

Mr. Watson-Harvey did not demand to see the Chief Constable. He said: "Who else is in authority?"

"I am."

"Then I demand—"

The heart was beating up under Rosher's durable blue serge. He was about to stick his neck out again, and he knew it. Prudence said: Don't. Don't do it—you're under the chopper already. The blood said: attack. Self-interest said: a reaction here—you'll have something to shove at Archie, at the Old Man—you may snatch salvation. Stern faced, he plunged. Blood will tell, in the end.

"Your daughter is a confessed felon, sir. You are in no position to demand anything." A bark, for the softening-up. And then—here went the fucking book, for the big one. "You might, of course, try bribery on the man with the keys. A packet of fivers might do it."

He got the reaction. Mr. Watson-Harvey came upright, stiff

on his unfriendly chair. Shock, that was, in his eyes. "What . . . what are you suggesting?" It sounded as though he had been running hard, with a fishbone in his throat.

The inspector's hunter-heart cried gladly: got him! Nab him—on suss. Which, translated, means suspicion. But prudence drew him back now. There is a world of difference between private knowing and public proof. If he dropped one here, he'd never get out from under. Be crafty. He said, with not a trace of laughter or twinkle about him: "A joke, sir. Inspired by another case I'm working on." He displayed the file. "A small printing firm. Strangely enough, young Poddy used to work there."

Mr. Watson-Harvey managed: "Poddy? He's dead."

"Yes. Quite true. So he can't tell us about it, can he? Never to worry—we'll soon be talking to somebody who can."

Mr. Watson-Harvey's face was a wax skull. He said on a panting breath: "You . . . you . . . know . . . you—" And then he rose up out of his chair; right up, clutching at his chest with a great, rasping gasp; and pitched forward, right across the little desk.

Oh, Jesus Christ! thought Rosher, springing forward. And when he found what condition Mr. Watson-Harvey was in: Oh, Jesus Fucking Christ!

For once—surely the only time in all his long career—he lost his cool. He jumped to the door; opened it and bellowed along toward Reception: "Barney—get an ambulance!"

But no ambulance would do any good now, for the man sprawled across the nasty little desk. Mr. Watson-Harvey was dead.

168

16

Nobody could blame Rosher for the death of Mr. Watson-Harvey. Nobody openly tried, although he had to answer questions, of course, put to him first by Superintendent Bishop when he came shooting out of his office, as other people shot from theirs, and galloped along to the interview room at Rosher's yell; and later by the Chief Constable. Archie, in the stress of the moment, jerked out the one that touched everybody's mind as the situation made impact. "You didn't touch him, did you?"

"'Course I bloody didn't," Rosher barked. "He fell down dead."

Postmortem proved that he had. Cardiac arrest, brought on no doubt by stress to be expected in view of the general circumstances. Not a bruise on the body, not a mark. So that was all right.

Only Mr. Rosher knew what took place between them in that nasty little room; and Mr. Rosher was not inclined to tell. He took Mr. Watson-Harvey in there, he said, because the man was clearly overexcited and about to stage a public scene in the reception hall. He had explained that Superintendent Bishop felt it would hamper investigations to permit visits to the daughter at present, and subject fell down dead. Just like that.

It made fresh headlines, of course, the editor of the local paper in particular sobbing with joy as he screamed for madder type and blacker ink; especially as there seemed no end to the bounty.

They had arrested a Mr. Gooch and the police were even now sweeping up all the little junkies and peddlars named by Fiona before they transferred her to the big city gaol. But from the police point of view, this aspect of the case was not so satisfactory. The city man vanished as soon as the media announced the arrest of the twins and Fiona, and efforts to trace supply back to source were unsuccessful. Cut-out points all the way.

They cleaned up a lot of the little people, though. Most of the disappointment was swallowed by the big city force and Scotland Yard, who took the job over from the town Drugs Squad when the trail led onward and, they'd hoped, upward. But Scotland Yard had some compensation in the matter of the forgery business. Mr. Gooch was just what their little hearts had long desired.

Mr. Gooch was the printer who came in to work for Mr. Watson-Harvey after he made the arrangement with three hard men from London. It did not take long—and Rosher gained badly needed kudos for this—to uncover the late (but only just) Mr. Watson-Harvey's printing interest. Archie Bishop sent out for copies of the business directories covering previous years, and there it was. His dropping the listing for this year looked odd. Either he had sold out—no trace of a new owner—or he wanted to lay the connection doggo.

The police moved before the fact of Mr. Watson-Harvey's death was known beyond the town station. A phone call is all they used, and a car to take the two Scotland Yard men to the scene. Silly buggers, they had come by train.

It was a nice little shop in the big city, right next door to Mr. Watson-Harvey's tea-importing firm. Wedding invitations in the window, samples of personal stationery, club fixture lists and everything. Mr. Gooch had just reached the door, headed for home, when he found himself bundled back in by burly men flashing warrant cards. Some minutes later he came out again and left in a car between two of them for a quite unexpected destination, the spare men following in a second car with the engraved plates, special paper brought from London in a smart executive case, and the

170

batch of genuine official inks. Very useful was Mr. Gooch, when he became talkative.

None of this activity involved the murder team. Chief Superintendent Bishop and Inspector Rosher had nothing at all to do with it once they had furnished the materials; for doing which, kudos accrued to all, as far down as Sergeant Panton; although in the inspector's case the shadow hung still. At the station they were not sure how to treat him, because it really did seem that young Timothy was quietly dying. Comatose, weakening, and being fed by unlikely methods. Medical science has made great strides since leeches.

It was two days before they could see Mrs. Watson-Harvey. And they had to see her, nobody so closely woven into such a web of almost incestuous villainy can expect to be left out of the inquiry altogether. There could be—there should be—connection between all the various villainies, considering the close contacts between the two families. She might well have been involved, if not as active participant, at least as accessory. To hubby only? Because her reaction suggested that Fiona's depredations came as complete, prostrating shock. Or on both hands, linking the two? Possibly, even, with neither husband or daughter knowing what the other was up to. She might even be able to shed light on the fate of young Poddy.

All highly unlikely. But so many things are. Look at the murdering disciples of Charles Manson. Look at Ma Barker, many fragrant years ago.

So two days later Superintendent Bishop and Inspector Rosher, told that it was now possible to interview her, set out into wild and windy weather. Not to Hutton Fellows, she had been kept in the hospital. Consider. In her state of collapse they could hardly send her back to the big house, all alone. With all the rubbernecks about, some of them actually creeping up the drive to peer at the place? One of their children, son of a Mr. and Mrs. Bert Whalley, come all the way from Nottingham, had already heaved a brick through a front window. Got clumped for it by his father, after the entire family had run like the clappers for the car; but that's not the point.

It is possible that Mrs. Watson-Harvey, in her collapsed condition, would have spilled everything she knew as readily as her daughter did, but for one inhibiting factor: the existence of that daughter, for whom she bore this inordinate love. Too much to say that she thought coherently into the matter, any kind of straight thinking was beyond her. But deeper than thought lies maternal love, and the greater the buffeting, the more unbalanced it grows. Who would strengthen and sustain the beloved—beloved, beloved, whatever she did and forever—if she herself were gone?

They saw her in one of the small lounges set aside for visitors. When she came in, ushered by a quiet nurse and wearing a plaid dressing gown too big for her, supplied by the hospital because there had been nobody at home to pack a small suitcase, Inspector Rosher thought: Christ.

Nobody now would have doubted that she was old enough to have a daughter of Fiona's age. No makeup on her stressed, bony face, hair lank and pinned back almost as Fiona's had been, she walked uncertainly, like an old woman. The dressing gown might even have fitted when she was brought here just a few days ago. Superintendent Bishop said, the gentleness in his tone showing his own shock: "Ah. Mrs. Watson-Harvey. Come in, come in. Do sit down. All right, nurse, we'll call you when we've finished."

"Thank you." Mrs. Watson-Harvey's voice was a near whisper. The nurse stayed with her until she was seated in one of the plastic-and-chrome, bright chairs. The whole room was bright, curtains, painted walls, rugs, the autumn flowers in colourful vases on low tables. Superintendent Bishop took another of the several chairs, leaning back with coat unbuttoned and his hat on his knee. Inspector Rosher remained standing, and buttoned up. But he'd taken his hat off. The super said:

"How are you feeling, Mrs. Watson-Harvey?"

"Very well. Thank you." Patently, she was not. But she told a brave lie.

"I'm sorry to have to ask you questions at a time like this but it is in everybody's interests. There are matters to be cleared up regarding your . . . Mr. Watson-Harvey's affairs." He paused. She said nothing. He carried on. "I believe he had printing interests. In the city, next door to his tea interests. Private printing." A good name. Some of the work was very private.

She looked at him; said after a silence, vaguely: "I . . . I'm sorry . . . I didn't . . . hear . . .?" The super repeated the question. She said: "I am afraid I know very little about my husband's business interests."

But she did—she knew about the printers. She had not known then what was being set up; but she presided at the little dinner—one of many cooked and hostessed to oil the wheels of trade—when the three hard men came from London. She had not liked them, and she never knew why they came; and this was not unusual, she did not concern her self with business. She had enough to worry about with the soufflé. She knew it had something to do with the printing business, though. He was thinking of expanding it, he told her later. "Really, dear?" she had said; not actually listening, because she was cutting up some of the cold meat for Rover.

"He had a printing firm, madam, I can assure you of that," the kindly-looking man was saying. Kindly-looking; but he was one of the chief causes why the beloved child was where she was. Why her husband was dead. Why *she* was where she was. The other man—the hard, gorilla one—looked the part.

"Did he?"

"I understand from your daughter that he employed young Edward Poddy there."

" . . . believe he did employ him . . . Teddy . . . for a time."

Oh yes—he employed Teddy. That was the great mistake. Took him on at Fiona's pleading, when she thought she would be marrying him. "He's *ever* so clever, Daddy—but you see, he hasn't been *trained* for anything." So George took him on, to handle office work and generally make himself useful; just to please her, really, and to have him under the eye. To watch how he performed. To see what happened to the Big Romance before committing himself to making something more solid and dignified. If only he had started him in the tea firm. Although there was nothing secret about the printing, then. George genuinely originally bought it as a business ripe for expansion, and to cut cost on printing necessary to his other interests.

"In the printing firm," the kindly man said.
"Yes. I believe so." Funny how the exhausted mind seizes on trivialities. That's a nice coat he's wearing, she thought.
Sergeant Rosher stirred. Initially, she had given the impression that she did not know there was a printing firm. Now, she believed young Poddy worked there. He would have chased the point up; but Archie was saying: "How long ago was that?"
"A year. About. Or a little more."

Before we found out she—the lovely, the innocent—had nearly married a lunatic. Long before *we* realised he was a lunatic—she knew; but she would not tell us why, when she came home so white and shaken to say she was finished with him. And George fired him.

"When did he leave, do you know?"
"No. He wasn't there long."
"Did your husband dismiss him, or did he just . . . leave?"
"I don't know. I believe he left. I don't really know."
"And that was last winter?"
"Yes."

And in the early spring he started—what he started.

"Did you see him after that?"

"No."

He vanished. From my life, and Fiona's. But not from
George's. He reappeared in his life, George said, in March.

"He went into hospital. In June."
"Yes. I believe he did."
"His . . . friendship . . . with your daughter. It was over, by
then?"
"Yes. When she . . . we . . . realised he was not . . .
suitable."
"And you didn't see him again? After he came out of hospital?"
"No."

Yes. Oh yes—I saw him again. Just once. Only once. A few
days, a lifetime ago. When George was alive—and Rover—and
Fiona was . . . a little girl. A second small matter crossed her
mind.
"What's happened to . . . Rockie? My daughter's horse."
"He's being taken care of. Don't worry." The kindly eyes
glanced at the standing gorilla-man. The gorilla-man said abruptly:
"On the farm next door. Mr. Adams. They're looking after
him."
"Thank you," she said.

Oh yes. I saw him. Fiona was out, gone on one of her outings
with her schoolfriend Nicky Plover, who lived in the city. An afternoon of shopping and gossip; an evening of dancing; to be home
by midnight, Rover to guard her. A sweet girl, Nicky Plover.
Mrs. Watson-Harvey was out, too. Or should have been. The
weekly Ladies Guild meeting, in the village hall. But a call went
up for somebody to take over the church flowers from old Miss
Spender, who had broken a hip. She volunteered.
She came out from the church with Mrs. Timmins, the village
woman rostered with Miss Spender to do the flowers, earlier than
she would have come from the meeting. It was still going on; but

with only half an hour left, she decided it was not worth going back. The evening speaker was only Mrs. Barnstable, showing her slides yet again. My Greek Holiday, proudly illustrated with badly taken snaps of islands which she knew herself better than Mrs. Barnstable did. The church is this side of the village hall, so she'd only have to walk down and all the way back again. She said goodnight to Mrs. Timmins and went home.

As soon as she entered the house she heard Teddy, raving in the kitchen. She moved to listen at the door; heard what he was saying, punctuated by the occasional deeper note of her husband's urgent protesting.

The nightmare followed, and had continued ever since. She did not remember—her mind had blanked out—much of what he said; but suddenly he was abusing Fiona. That is what took her into the kitchen, this filthy-tongued attack on her beloved child.

George was at the table, wearing the ridiculous pinafore he donned when he cut up meat for Rover. The dog would eat, when he came in. He looked ghastly, white and shaken, the red meat on the board and the knife lying beside it. Teddy stood at a distance, mouthing his filth. She did not know until the press said so that there were drugs working in him. She thought he was gone over the top again. As he was; and further than ever, because of the drugs.

He turned on her. As soon as she came in. Her arrival did not even disrupt the flow. A spate of filth. He said that Fiona—and the twins—and with him—and anybody. She moved closer to George.

Then he began on her. Nice tits, he said, he'd always fancied them. And he'd have 'em, he'd have her like he'd had her randy daughter. . . .

This is when George moved. Because Teddy was coming forward, impelled toward her by his raving vehemence. He moved—George did—and was suddenly locked with the boy; was behind him, trying to pin his arms, the lad's struggling body upright before her. She hardly remembered picking up the knife. She remembered George's shout: "No. No," and his whispered: "Oh my Christ," when Teddy had sagged to the floor.

They should have done better than bundle him into the car boot to dump him in the quarry. Perhaps if they had told the police that he simply appeared and attacked them—he had a history of mental illness— And there were drugs in him.

But they didn't know about the drugs, then. And Fiona would be home. Fiona must not know—she must never know—her parents—her mother—did this.

They were not seasoned killers. They panicked.

It was dark, thank God, and nobody was likely to be about at night on the lane that runs past the rear of the house to and on through the woods, at the back of which the quarry lies. O God— they got Teddy out from the boot and along the path, leaving the car where it was screened by bushes from all around. A regular parking spot, used by tourists in summer. They got him well into the wood; but George—it was very dark—whispered that he'd missed the path leading off to the quarry. The quarry it had to be; there were holes in the abandoned face, there were rocks to be rolled—he knew it, from walking with Rover.

"Stay here," he whispered. "I'll have to check."

"I can't . . . I can't . . . " she said.

"Stay here!" The sheer strain in him snapped at her; and he was moving away. And then, with Teddy on the ground, they heard the somebody coming. Whistling along the path, just 'round the bend. And she, with a terified sob, found herself running. At her shoulder George, sobbing his own panic.

Perhaps if she had not run—if George had not been at a distance—they might have got into the bushes—waited until the whistler went by— Oh well.

One piece of luck they had: in their panic, George had actually gone in his slippers. No press report had mentioned tracks, so presumably they left no mark. And she herself had run on leaves, away from the path. There'd be plenty of tracks about, of course, if they lasted this long from the tourist season.

When they got home she cleaned the blood from the kitchen floor, while George stuffed into the boiler whatever had been in the car boot. His sweater, too, went in, there was blood on that.

The knife she put back in the drawer. Fiona would miss it otherwise, when she came to prepare Rover's midday dinner tomorrow. Missing it, she would ask questions. It was still there, wiped clean and used since. It had horrified her, to see Fiona handling it.

"Do you know," the kindly-looking policeman was saying, "of any way he could have got money from your husband? We are thinking in terms of blackmail."

"No."

"He seems to have acquired some ten thousand pounds. Mr. Watson-Harvey's fingerprints are on the notes."

"I don't know anything about that."

Not in any great detail. I was not hearing very well. And Fiona was coming home. And you were not being very clear, George, when you told me, after we finished the cleaning. When we were drinking the enormous brandies. And after—when Fiona came home, and ever since—by some unspoken collusion, we never spoke of it again. Not even when we were alone together. Somehow, we resmoothed the surface of life, we acted as though it never happened.

He had told her of businesses recession-hit and tottering, where she had never given a thought to them, believing them safe. Of two or three truckloads of tea—of all innocuous beverages— offered by a man in London, when he was there on one of his working trips, very cheap. Delivered into his warehouse, cash down and no questions asked. Of the initial blackmail by the man, one of those who later came to dinner, coercing him into using the printing firm for forgery. And he needed money: for you, he said, and for Fiona. The house, the way of life. . . . The other businesses—the recession—no end in sight—

He told her of Teddy coming back to break into the print shop after he had been fired—George didn't know how, but Teddy had a friend, that Tom Nolan, skilled in housebreaking. Of his appearing in March, to demand regular payment. Large payment—and he possessed a packet of the forgeries, to back the demands.

And then Teddy went into hospital, and George thought perhaps. . . . So he stopped the payments. But Teddy came out; and last week George got a note, couched in weird terms, he said, saying he would be calling.

He thought, George did, that he meant he would call at the office, as usual; but he suddenly arrived at home. Came in by the back door—it was never locked until they went to bed. Said he came to . . . to . . . with Fiona. Said he wanted his money. He was mad. Oh, he was mad. But sane enough, presumably, to have watched her going, to make sure she was out of the way. He'd have thought—if what ran in his head was thought—that Fiona was home. When he found that she wasn't, George said, he went completely wild.

"I presume you know your husband was producing forged notes?"

"No. No, I . . . . No. I didn't know."

Not much of a reaction, Inspector Rosher thought. Mind you, she's pretty knocked out. What's one more shock? If it is a shock. Superintendent Bishop was speaking again.

"I'm afraid he was. And it seems that the Wellington twins were passing them for him."

Now her eyes flicked; and the flick registered in Rosher's mind. "I don't know anything about my husband's . . . business ventures," she said.

And she didn't, in detail. Mr. Watson-Harvey had not told her about the twins, for a very good reason. He didn't know. It was all set up without his knowing. Even the tea was part of the set-up—it was offered because he was Fiona's father.

Things like drugs and forgery capers are very carefully engineered. The men in London were deeply into both. They needed a small out-of-town printing facility run by a respectable somebody. So they put the buzz about.

One of their own men came up with Mr. Watson-Harvey—the drug peddlar who already had Fiona on his book; and the perfect go-between for distribution, too—twins, no impediments, living alone more or less in a house easy of access and private. Game for anything, if there was money in it.

So they offered Mr. Watson-Harvey the tea; and he bit. They never told him they owned Fiona—she was held in reserve, for use if he cut up later. All he had to do, they said, was employ their man for the printing. That's all. Big money in it.

And that is all he had to do. Mr. Gooch himself delivered the funnies to the twins, who, in their turn, never knew they came from Mr. Watson-Harvey. Cut-out points, you see, every step of the way. Nobody knowing more than they had to. The big boys in London are masters of the art.

"On the night when Mr. Poddy was killed, where was Mr. Watson-Harvey?"

"At home. With me."

"All the evening?"

"I was in church for a short time. Doing the flowers."

You should push that, Rosher thought. But the Archbishop sat for a moment in silence before he said: "Well, thank you, madam. We won't bother you anymore, at this time. A sad business. Very."

He was stirring. He was rising, buttoning up his coat. The lady looked up at him, swathed in the plaid wool dressing gown. Even her ankles, visible between nightdress hem and the borrowed slippers, were gone bony. She murmured: "Thank you. Thank you very much."

"I will send the nurse back in, as we go out. Good day to you."

They left her there and went back through the hospital smell to the reception hall, and out. Nobody else they needed to see. Mrs. Wellington was gone, to a nursing home. Young Timothy, they knew before they left the station, was not expected to last much longer. If he'd lasted this far. When they were in the car, the inspector said: "I think she knows a lot more about it than she's telling."

180

"Uh-huh," said the Archbishop. "I don't doubt it. Could very well be. What's the point in shoving it? We can't do any more to her—she's finished. Sleeping dog—let it lie. I'll have a word with the Old Man, when we get back."

"Er-rrrer," said Rosher. "Grrrrmph."

As soon as they reached the station, Archie Bishop went up alone to the Chief Constable's office. They were closeted for some ten minutes before the intercom buzzed on Inspector Rosher's desk, to summon him.

"Ah," said the Chief, when he came in. "Mr. Rosher. Good. Splendid. I have been hearing from Mr. Bishop about your visit to Mrs. Watson-Harvey. Sad business, very sad. I knew them, you know. Not well, but I always looked upon them as very decent people."

He paused. Rosher said: "Uh-huh." The Chief went on.

"I want to personally congratulate you, and everybody concerned in the case. I think—we all do, of course, Mr. Bishop does, and no doubt you will agree—that Edward Poddy's death can be imputed to the Wellington twins. Unfortunately we have no actual witnesses—no firm proof—and it seems no chance of getting any. But we are quite justified in counting the matter as cleared. The other matters, of course—splendid. They are nicely under control. Scotland Yard has been very complimentary."

"Uh-huh."

Archie spoke. "Good work, Alf." Fancy that—called him Alf.

"It appears," said the Chief, "that your young man will never be able to tell us anything. About anything. I . . . er . . . I have been speaking with our doctor. He has . . . conferred . . . with the hospital doctor. They are agreed that any injuries sustained by the patient were quite obviously . . . er . . . inflicted . . . when he fell. While he was holding the gun. Struck his . . . head . . . his jaw . . . on the edge of the table, or something. You did say there was a table?"

"Yes, sir." Oh, the stance of the man, bowed legs braced,

181

long arms dangling, short-back-and-sides head lowered between the burly shoulders.

"Yes. Well, good. Splendid. Thank you, Mr. Rosher, that will be all."

"Thank you, sir," said Rosher. One hand had moved to his pocket, he was bringing out the dreaded handkerchief.

The Chief's deep courtesy wavered at last. "If you are going to blow your nose," he snapped acidly, "oblige me by doing it outside."

"Ah," the inspector said. "Rmmph. Grmph." He turned away. The door closed behind him.

Immediately, from outside came the frenetic rending of insane calico. The Chief winced; sighed; looked up to find a twinkle in the superintendent's eye, an upward twitching at the corners of his mouth. Suddenly, both men found themselves rocking, helpless with laughter.

"Oh dear, oh dear," said the Chief when he was able, wiping his eyes on a handkerchief spotless as befitted his rank and domestic situation. "There's never a dull moment, is there, with our Mr. Rosher around."

"We should have stood him on the steps when we saw the Scotland Yard lads off," gurgled the Archbishop. "He could have blown one of those at 'em as they left."

Collapse again, of both stout parties.